My Big Heart-Shaped Fail

My Big Heart-Shaped Fail

Award-winning author of *Just Add Magic* and *Saltwater Secrets*

CINDY CALLAGHAN

SPARKPRESS

Published by SparkPress, a BookSparks imprint,
A division of SparkPoint Studio, LLC
Phoenix, Arizona, USA, 85007
www.gosparkpress.com

Published 2022
Printed in the United States of America
Print ISBN: 978-1-68463-161-2

E-ISBN: 978-1-68463-162-9

Library of Congress Control Number: 2022904052

Interior design by Tabitha Lahr

DEDICATION

To all the middle-school girls who've experienced a totally, utterly cringe-worthy day. I promise, it will pass.

CHAPTER 1

Secrets, lies, and friends don't go together.

Paige, Jess, and I have been a trio forever—"PaigeJess AndAbby." All one word. That is, until it started feeling like "PaigeAndJess" "AndAbby." I thought it was their fault, but it was me. I had a secret that I couldn't tell them—the kind that could tear a friendship apart.

❤ ❤ ❤

I walked out of Mount Lebanon Middle School with Jess on one side and Paige on the other. The smell of one week of freedom floated among the flurries in the air.

Winter break.

Since third grade, we'd spent winter break together. Every year we'd made a "Winter Break Bucket List" of all the things we'd do together during the week. It started off as princess dress-ups and indoor s'mores, then we graduated to blanket forts and indoor s'mores, then on to snowmen and indoor s'mores, and last year we ambushed the boys from school with snowballs and, of course, we made indoor s'mores. It was during that snowball battle that I fell for my crush. Well, first I fell *on* him, and then I fell *for* him. Unfortunately, I'd fallen on/for a guy I could never tell my friends about.

But this year, winter break would be different. For the first time, we wouldn't be together. Paige was visiting her grandma, while Jess had signed up for the week-long, school-sponsored snow-tubing trip, and I'd been accepted to University of Delaware's winter STEM program for eighth graders. It was my video application that got me in. . . . Paige played the role of Absolute Zero, and Jess was Pi.

The three of us sat on the frozen bench and waited for the school bus. The cold seeped through my jeans and chilled me to the bone. We pushed close together to keep warm, creating a literal visualization of PaigeJessAndAbby.

Paige pulled a glove off with her teeth, read her texts, and announced, “I have news.”

We perked up. It was probably a big decision about her next DIY project. Last week’s homemade glitter had sparkled in my hair until yesterday.

She said, “I’m not going to my grandma’s. She booked a Caribbean cruise for herself. Can you believe it?”

“That’s exciting for her!” Jess said. “Who knew Gram was such a jet-setter?”

“Good for Grammy, but what are you gonna do?” I asked.

“Seems the options are limitless.” She looked at me. “Or limited—I guess it depends on how you look at it. I’d never get into the STEM program, as much as I’d love to stay in one of those new dorms.”

Paige’s eyes lit up as she continued, “But I’m going to . . .” She looked at Jess.

“Don’t say it,” Jess said. “Don’t you dare say it.” She paused. “Go ahead. Say what I think you’re going to say, but you had better say what I hope you’re gonna say. Just sayin’.”

“I’m going on the tubing trip! Eeek!”

“With me?” Jess asked.

"With *you*!" Paige said. "A group of kids got the flu and dropped out. My mom got me in!"

They squealed and did their best to hug through their puffy winter coats. They would have the best winter break ever. I mean, *we* would have the best winter breaks ever. Mine at UD and theirs on the school's tubing trip . . . together. They would be together in the mountains, and I wouldn't be there.

I pushed a smile to show my excitement for them.

Paige read my face. "Oh, I'm sorry, Ab. Are you mad?"

Inside I was saying: "I'm not mad, but I'm totally jealous that you guys are going away without me, and I'm worried that you're going to come back as besties with each other and you won't need me anymore."

Instead, I said: "Me? No. No way. You guys will have a great time. That's awesome."

"It gets better," Paige said.

Jess's eyes sparkled. "Oooo, tell me."

I echoed with my own forced enthusiasm, "What could be better than that?"

Paige paused for dramatic effect, then said, "Tao's going—" Tao was Paige's boyfriend. They were like that uber-popular, uber-good-looking boyfriend-girlfriend pair that everyone envied. Tao was an awesome guy who was friends with everyone. "—and Ben!"

Jess squealed again. Recently Jess had informed us that she liked Ben. "For real?"

Paige confirmed, "They were on the waiting list and they got in."

Jess stood up and clapped her mittened hands together. "Ben!"

Jess said to me, "When we get back, we're going to work on a boyfriend for you."

Paige added, "Yes. Just in time for the dance. We'll triple-date."

I said, "That sounds great," but I didn't mean it.

Then Jess tugged me and Paige off the bench and put an arm over each of our shoulders. "I wish you were going with us, Ab."

"Me too," Paige said.

"But here's the thing with best friends—we're always together even when we're apart." Jess patted her heart through the thick down coat. "Right here." She was goofy-serious.

"Always. We're stuck like glue. Gorilla Glue, of course, and sprinkled with glitter and wrapped in a raffia bow." Then Paige added, "Pink."

"Well, obvi," I said. Paige had perfectly described what I wanted forever: PaigeJessAndAbby glued, glittered, and raffia-ed in pink.

They pulled me into a group hug, but things already felt different, like it was *their* group hug that they'd pulled me into.

The huddle broke up when the bus arrived. The three of us squeezed into one seat.

Manny got on and walked past us. "Have fun at UD, Abs."

"Thanks, Manny."

No doubt I'd have fun immersed in STEM for a week, but I also had a serious case of FOMO, and there wasn't even anything to miss yet.

When Manny was in his seat in the back, Jess asked me, "How about Manny?"

"What about him?" I asked. Manny and I had been friends since second grade. We were neighbors, and our moms were friends.

Jess clarified, "For the dance."

"Yeah. The triple date. Good idea," Paige said.

Since I could never go to the dance with my real crush, I said, "Maybe."

One Week Later

CHAPTER 2

Jess's bedroom was the best: four-poster bed, plasma screen TV, and an amazing, overstuffed walk-in closet. She shared everything in it with me and Paige.

"Your look on the first day back from winter break is essentially your brand for the rest of the school year," Jess advised.

Paige went for "matchy-matchy" in winter-white jeans and sweater that really popped against her dark skin.

"How about these earrings?" Jess held up a pair of snowflake chandeliers for Paige.

"Nah. Too big for me," Paige said.

"There's nothing wrong with the ones you're wearing, but these will pull the whole look together."

Paige felt her little pearl studs. "I like these."

"Me too," Jess said, "but these are better. Just sayin'."

That was so Jess. She would say something unfiltered and add "just sayin'," almost like an apology. Here's the thing: she wasn't mean; she was honest. Usually "just sayin'" ended the conversation.

Jess had landed on black skinny jeans, boho top, and wool cap over her long, balayaged, straight brown hair. "This look says 'totally playful.'"

I eyed my pile of rejections on the floor around me, not sure what I wanted my brand to say.

Our school, "The Mount," had an ecosystem in which everyone had a label. Mine? Smart girl. Specifically, math. Luckily, it was all on-trend to be STEM-y, because the thing with labels was once you had one, it stuck. Poor Gordon Chang picked his nose in kindergarten, and he'd forever been known as Nosepicker Gordon. So how did the on-trend smart girl dress to reflect her brand?

Then it started . . . what I'd worried would happen:

"Oh, Paige, remember the time we mixed up the body parts of everyone's snowmen?" Through a snorty laugh, Jess added, "Abby, it was hysterical. We put a girly wig on the one with the suit vest and a tiara on the one that was supposed to be Chewbacca."

They burst out laughing. I did too, to join in, but it was sort of like you had to be there. Inside jokes were awkward when you weren't inside.

Paige's eyes were tearing up. "Oh, okay, *Jazzy* . . ."

At that, Jess laughed harder. She told me, "That was my nickname during break." And she showed me her jazz hands. Then to Paige she said, "Right, *Paigey*?"

Paige bent over to hold her belly as she squealed at that. Although "Paigey" didn't sound like a particularly funny nickname, I giggled about it.

> ***I wanted to say:*** "I had a fun winter break too. I had a nickname too, 'Abacus,' get it?"

But I thought it would need explaining, and then it wouldn't be funny anymore. It was also awkward having an inside joke when you were the only person inside.

They talked about the lodge, the firepit, s'mores, and sled dogs. Sometimes they'd pause to give a little explanation. The pinging and ponging conversation got faster.

"We made snow angels—"

"Wiped out on the hill—"

"A sheet of ice—"

"It was hilarious—"

"I was dying—"

> ***I wanted to say:*** "And this kid told a joke about a farmer who had one hundred ninety-six cows, but when he rounded them up, he had two hundred. Get it? Round *up*? It was soooo funny."

But this was no time for a math joke.

My week had been awesome too, but different from theirs. I'd made a bunch of new friends who I was keeping in touch with on InstaPic, and I'd really loved working through long, complicated equations on a whiteboard with colored dry-erase markers. It was a level of math I could never get at school. I'd figured they wouldn't understand how my brain had found its happy place. Then I'd received texts from Paige and Jess from the trip, and those had made me less happy. First, there were selfies of the two of them. By the second day, the pics included Ben and Tao. By day three, they were all "coupley."

I could feel it happening while they'd been tubing. PaigeAndJess was moving away from AndAbby.

Now, here in Jess's closet, the distance was clear. Every sentence cracked my heart a little.

I'd made a plan for this, but thinking it over, maybe it was a bad plan. I didn't think I could actually do it.

Jess said, "Oh, Abby, on the last day we did the most amazing thing. We each wrote down one thing we regretted from the trip."

Paige added, "We kept it a secret. And then we ceremoniously tossed it into the firepit so we could end the week with no regrets."

Jess said, "It was totally cleansing."

"Wow, a cleansing ceremony, how very . . . campy. Sounds great." I tried to sound like I believed it was great, but come on, how dumb. Besides, what could they possibly regret?

Paige said, "It was a perfect way to end the week."

"Perfect," Jess added.

Then the topic shifted to the boys.

"And then me and Tao . . ."

"There was one time that Ben . . ."

"The fireworks on the ski hill were so romantic . . ."

"So romantic . . ."

Then Paige said, "That's when Tao kissed me for the first time."

I had to make this stop.

I wrung my hands as I wondered again about my plan. Maybe it wasn't so bad.

Could I?

Should I?

Then they sighed in unison about the kiss.

The sigh did it.

I said what I'd planned: "I met an awesome guy last week."

Talk about regrets—as soon as the words were out of my mouth, I regretted making the plan and going through with it. They fired questions at me:

"You did?" Jess asked.

"Why didn't you say so?" Paige asked.

"I just did. Just now."

"Well." Jess opened her arms. "Do tell."

And my plan unfolded like the pile of clothes on the floor of Jess's closet.

"His name is Fabio Risotto."

"He's shy . . ."

"Cute . . ."

"Loves math . . ."

"Held my hand . . ."

With each colorful detail I added, they listened closer than they ever would've if I was talking about quadratic equations, coding, or derivatives.

Then something else happened, something I hadn't planned—I couldn't stop. The harder they listened, the more my mouth moved.

"Oh, we went to the Rainbow Freaks concert," I said. Even Fabio wouldn't be able to get tickets to the Rainbow Freaks.

"No way," Paige said.

Jess said, "I'm so jelly."

"We went backstage and got the drummer's autograph." *Why did I have to add that?*

"You did not," Paige said.

Jess said, "I'm obsessed with the Rainbow Freaks."

I didn't want to lie, but I couldn't control the word vomit pouring out of my mouth, because with each lie I felt "AndAbby" move closer to "PaigeAndJess."

Before I knew it, I'd bought boots I could never afford, and my family had booked a trip to Aruba for Thanksgiving.

In a matter of a few minutes on Jess's closet floor, things had gone *way* beyond my plan, admittedly a stupid plan.

I figured maybe it wasn't so bad—I could lose the boots, I'd never speak of the concert again, and Aruba could be canceled. But Fabio . . . The girls were totally curious.

"When can we meet him?" *Can you believe he lives all the way in Maine?*

"Can we see his profile?" *He hates social media.*

"Let's FaceTime him." *Good idea, but he's shy, so let's ease into that. Maybe another day.*

Unbeknownst to Fabio, one day soon we'd break up, but right now I needed him to Gorilla Glue me to the trio and to help me hide my real crush from the girls.

CHAPTER 3

It was killing me.

I flipped through my camera roll of pics of PaigeJess AndAbby from before winter break, and I replayed my UD admission video.

My lies and secret crush boiled inside me at 212 degrees Fahrenheit—if I didn't come clean, I'd boil over. But a confession would surely make me "AndAbby."

That's when I scrolled to one of the pictures the girls had sent me from the lodge—the firepit. I remembered the No Regrets Ceremony. I wanted to hate everything they'd done that week, but the more I thought about it, the more I thought there was something to this.

Using my best calligraphy, which Paige had taught me how to do, I made a list of confessions. The first one started: "*My heart aches*." Then I wrote one about lying to my friends and one about how I'd made up Fabio. Finally, I revealed my secret crush. Maybe there was something to this No Regrets thing, because writing these down made me feel better.

I cut the list into five small notes, folded them into origami frogs, and stuffed them deep in my pocket. Now I just needed to think of a way to ceremoniously destroy them.

CHAPTER 4

The next day, the decoration committee scoured Karleigh's Party Emporium for an epic selection of decorations to transform the gym for tomorrow night's dance, "Peppermint Twist."

I imagined what the dance would be like:
Jess and Ben in matching red-and-white gingham plaid. Paige and Tao in red-and-white polka dots.

So cute.

Jess says, "Where's Fabio?"

I say, "Snowstorm in Maine. He's not gonna make it."

Paige says, "Bummer."

Back in reality, the party store lady said to us, "Hey, girls, no one picked up these balloons. A shame, they're the biodegradable kind. And so pretty. You're welcome to them, if you like."

"I love balloons. That's why I'm so super-excited about the archway for the gym. I can't wait to walk through it with Tao. Can I have the pink one?" Paige asked.

"I'll take a purple one. Ben loves purple. How about you, Abby?" Jess asked.

The mention of these balloons gave me an idea as perfect as a polynomial multiplied by itself!

"Yes!" I said. "Can I have the red ones?"

"All five?" the lady asked.

"Please. If that's okay."

"Sure. I can't use them." The lady handed them to me and began ringing up our order.

"How long do you think they'll float?" I asked.

She looked at the clock. "Maybe an hour or two. They've been sitting around for a little while."

I held up my phone in different directions and made a show of saying, "Ugh. I can't get a signal in here. I don't want to miss anything on InstaPic." My signal was fine. I just wanted to get outside alone.

Jess looked at her phone. "My signal's fine. Thank you, cell towers! I'd never want to miss a pic. That would be the absolute worst."

"The worst," Paige confirmed as she gave the school's credit card information to pay the lady for the dance decorations.

"I'll meet you outside," I said.

Letting the five secrets that were stuffed deep down in my pocket float away on balloon strings would be totally symbolic.

As soon as the cold winter air bit at my cheeks, I clicked my weather app. Winds were southeast, and the parking lot was clear of obstacles, giving the balloons enough time to rise above the tree line before soaring toward the state forest. At six miles per hour, with one to two hours of float time remaining, they would drop six to twelve miles away in the dense woods, where my confessions would biodegrade long before the spring thaw.

Perfect.

I glanced back into the store at Paige and Jess, who were preoccupied with confetti. I quickly tied each confession to the string of a red balloon. One last glance confirmed that Paige and Jess were distracted by piñatas, and ceremoniously

I

let

the

balloons

float

away.

I felt my regret soar away with them.

❤ ❤ ❤

A moment later, Paige and Jess came out of the store pushing a cart full of dance decor.

"I made a detailed schedule. If we stick to it, we should be able to finish by the end of the school day tomorrow. I already spoke with Mr. Valdez about us missing class. The balloon arch should be delivered in the morning. Everything is going to be beautiful. The food will be delicious, and the decorations will be absolutely, positively, exactly perfect. That's the mission of this committee: beautiful, delicious, perfect," Paige said.

Truthfully, that was Paige's mission in life. Everything she touched became be-dazzled, be-glittered, be-laced, be-scented-markered, or otherwise crafted to perfection. She baked from scratch, and since she was in every club at school, everyone had tasted her creations. The consensus was that each item tasted as good as it looked.

"Right, committee?" Paige asked.

By "committee," she meant Jess and me. We always supported one another's endeavors.

"Right," I agreed.

Jess reached into her oversized leather purse and took out a lipstick. While applying it, she said, "With you at the helm, Paigey, it'll be like a peppermint utopia."

Paige smiled at the compliment.

Jess handed me the lipstick. "You might want a touch-up, Abs." She was tying her balloon around her wrist when she noticed mine was gone. "Oh, bummer. You lost your balloons. That checkout lady will probably give you another one. She dresses like she's lost in an outdated issue of *Allure*, but she seemed nice."

Paige and I looked at Jess like what she'd just said wasn't nice.

"What? She does. I'm just sayin'."

"Not everyone is up on the latest fashion trends like you," Paige said.

"How could they be?" She zipped her purse shut. "Hey, let's hit the Coffee Station. If I don't get a tall decaf vanilla caramel mocha latte with low-fat whipped cream raspberry swirl and a cherry on top, in a recycled cup with an extra layer of cardboard wrap, a plastic lid, and a thin straw, I'm gonna pass out."

> ***I imagined going to the Coffee Station:*** "I'll have a café Fibonoccé." The barista would look at me, puzzled. "You know, like 'Fibonacci'—a sequence of numbers in which every number

> after the first two is the sum of the two preceding ones." Workers and customers would laugh and laugh at my imperfect math rhyme.
>
> ***In reality,*** I knew no one would get the joke. That was the tough thing about having a mind that was mathy. People didn't always get me.

"Yeah. I'll get the same," Paige said.

"I'm gonna add an extra shot of espresso and cookie dough marshmallows to mine," I said. "Let's go before we're hypoglycemic."

"Does Fabio like cookie dough marshmallows?" Paige asked.

"Uh, sure," I said. Fabio liked whatever I said he liked.

As we walked to the Coffee Station, I looked over my shoulder at the five balloons floating away.

A soul free of regret felt good. Starting now, I was done lying. My secrets would fade into the distant universe of the state park, and everything would be great.

Or so I thought.

The Next Day

8:00am

CHAPTER 5

The temperature dived below zero and snow flurries whirled, but my mom braved the cold and helped me haul boxes of decorations into school.

"Thanks," I said as she dropped a bag from the Donut Hole into the last box. The Hole was right next to the school, and like most kids, we often stopped and grabbed breakfast on our way to school.

My math teacher, Mr. Valdez, pulled his pickup truck into the parking lot. Mom waved and flashed him her signature smile, which she always had even when she was tired from working late into the night.

She kissed her hand and touched my cheek with it. As she left, she called to Mr. Valdez, "Have a nice day."

He waved to her with his free hand, while the other fiddled with his car's antenna.

I called to him, "Everything okay over there?"

"Yup." He put something in his pocket, walked over to me, and put a red ribbon into my box. "Here, I think maybe you or someone dropped this."

"Uh, thanks," I said, but I hadn't been near his car, so I didn't see how I could've dropped it there. Maybe a stray piece of ribbon blew over.

"Go on inside before you freeze," he said, his eyes following my mom's car as it pulled out.

❤ ❤ ❤

It was impossible not to notice the school office, since it was overflowing with balloons. A delivery guy walked in behind me with another bunch.

"I'll take those," I offered, and towed a bunch of balloons to the gym along with my box. It was going to take a lot of trips to transport the rest of the delivery from the office.

Jess and Paige had started early and already striped one entire wall with red and white streamers. It looked great, like peppermint sticks, except they'd made ten stripes, while peppermint sticks had eleven, my favorite of all the prime numbers. I figured I'd add one more stripe later when no one was around. There was no need to be inaccurate.

Paige beamed at the balloons. "Yay! They're here." She looked behind me, and the smile drained from her face. "Where's the guy?"

"What guy?" I asked.

"Didn't the party store send a balloon-arch-maker guy?"

"No guy," I said.

Logan Murphy swaggered in behind me. "I'm a guy." This was the understatement of the trimester. Logan wasn't just any guy. He was Mount Lebanon Middle School's "It Guy." Logan worked in the school office on his free periods, like now, which gave him access to hall passes . . . At The Mount, hall passes were gold.

"Hi, Abby," he said to me without a hint of flirtation, yet I felt my cheeks blush.

All the girls at The Mount liked Logan. So far, he hadn't asked anyone to the dance, and lots of girls were holding out in hopes he'd ask them.

"How's it going?" I asked.

Before he could answer, Jess said, "Well, that's not gonna work. Logan can't build a balloon arch. He couldn't even build an Egyptian pyramid out of Legos in Social Studies."

Logan said, "Legos are rectangles and pyramids are triangles, so it's not as easy as it sounds."

As if Jess hadn't heard his defense, she said to me and Paige, "Look, he might have an awesome smile and be captain of the basketball team, but he is *not* a balloon arch builder. We need a professional." Then, she added, "Just sayin'."

Logan didn't seem offended. "You don't have to apologize for thinking I have an awesome smile. I get that a lot." He showed off the famous grin. Geez, he was cute.

"Okay," Paige said. "Slight problem with the *crème de la crème* of our decorations. And as chairwoman, I have a solution. We're going to make this arch ourselves with directions I'm going to download and print right now."

Nothing would stand in the way of Paige Bakenya transforming this gym into a Peppermint Twist dance wonderland.

"Okay, committee, stripe the next wall. I'll be back before you can say 'peppermint.'" With that, she took the one coveted hall pass Mr. Valdez had given us for the day.

"I'll let you girls handle this stripe business," Logan said, "and I'll get more balloons from the office."

"Paige just took the hall pass," Jess said.

He chuckled. "Dude, it's me. I navigate these halls like a stealth weapon." On his way out, he was decked by Chloe, who entered the gym dancing and singing.

"What the heck?" Logan asked, picking himself up and wiping gym floor dust off his basketball shorts—yeah, he wore shorts all winter. So cool.

Chloe ignored him. "He likes me!" she said and twirled.

"Uh, yeah, I'm so outta here." Logan left the gym.

"Who?" Jess and I asked.

Chloe said, "Tao."

WTW? Paige's Tao?

This was shocking. So shocking that I couldn't get words out to ask for clarification.

Chloe continued pirouetting, as if she were in a magical love trance. "I love love. Don't you?"

Luckily, Paige wasn't around to hear this, because she would've choked on her Peppermint Twist planner at the idea that her boyfriend, who she'd recently kissed for the first time, liked Chloe. This was so Chloe to stir up drama.

Jess asked, "What are you talking about?"

"You heard me right. Sorry for your friend Paige—actually, sorry, I'm not sorry—but here's the harsh reality, Jessica Sawyer: Tao likes *me*."

Lots of girls were jealous of Paige. She was pretty, was friendly to new kids, handed in assignments early, and had the best-decorated locker. She always shared her homemade cookies with everyone, and somehow they always seemed to be fresh out of the oven, even when it was late in the day. It was a mystery no one had ever been able to solve.

"Everyone knows Tao and Paige are boyfriend and girlfriend. Where did you even get this idea? I'm just sayin', the idea is ridiculous." Sometimes Jess not having a filter was good, because it got her point out in the open rather than beating around the bush.

"Ridiculous, you say? Then why did he give me *this*?" Chloe held up a paper that Jess snatched and read to herself. When she was done, she handed it to me. But I didn't have to read it.

I already knew what it said, because Tao hadn't written it.

I had.

CHAPTER 6

My stomach knotted so tight I thought I might puke. Instantly my pulse increased. I'd read about this in one of my mom's magazines: Arrhythmia: A sudden irregular heartbeat, too fast or too slow. Mine was definitely too fast right now.

I looked at the note in my hand.

How could this happen?

"I don't believe it," I said.

"Believe it, Abby Gray." Chloe stopped dancing, jutted out a hip, and crossed her arms in front of her, which tugged her shirt up above the waistline of her jeans, revealing a sliver of white midriff in desperate need of sun.

My mouth was dry, and I could feel my face reddening. "Where did you get this?" I managed to ask through a forced smile.

"I just told you. From Tao! He tossed it to me in math this morning."

"Tossed it?" Jess asked. "Like how? Define 'tossed.'"

"You know, like a throw. He made it look all nonchalant. Isn't that cute? It landed right at my feet, and I was all, 'What's this?'"

Then she read: "*My heart aches to be so much in love and not be able to tell you.*"

I cringed at the words, so melodramatic, so gushy. Yuck. Thankfully, no one would ever know I'd written them or who they were about.

How had I so terribly miscalculated the landing of notes ceremoniously floating on balloon strings southeasterly at six miles per hour?

Then I thought about the equation. Maybe *I* hadn't been wrong. Maybe the lady at the store had underestimated the hours of float remaining and there'd been enough for them to soar over the entire state park. And, if one balloon landed, the others could too—with my notes attached.

It wouldn't take an honor roll student to connect the dots that would lead to me.

Everyone would learn about my secrets. They would figure out who I ached for. And my social life at The Mount would explode into a mushroom cloud of confetti that would fall in slush to get stepped on and eventually wash away.

I couldn't let that happen. I needed to redo the math to predict where others might have fallen and intercept them.

I imagined my brain was operating on Mach speed with Jeopardy! music playing in the background:

% . . .

Take the decimal to the hundredths . . .

. . .

Carry the two . . .

≤ . . .

÷ . . .

If x, then y . . .

YES!

My mental image continued:

I smash the *Jeopardy!* buzzer. "I've got it! What is 'the location of the fallen balloons'?"

I run like a jaguar, snatching up my notes just before they hit the ground, zip into the school cafeteria's kitchen, and shove them in the garbage disposal.

If it turns out that Mount Lebanon Middle doesn't have a garbage disposal, I'll fly into the science lab and toast them under the open flame of a Bunsen burner.

No Bunsen burners ignited? I'll bolt through the concrete block walls to the art room, where I'll decoupage the notes to oaktag and cover them generously with black poster paint. *Voila*: a modern art masterpiece that could hang anywhere, and no one would ever know the contents of the papers.

But what my mind actually did was:

Add or multiply first?

∞ . . .

Macaroni . . .

♫ . . .

🤦‍♀️ . . .

ã . . .

🥺 . . .

I had to calm down.

I remembered something else from one of my mom's magazines: Deep Breathing.

I inhaled 1-2-3.

And exhaled 3-2-1.

Inhaled 1-2-3.

It worked.

A few breaths and my brain could work again.

What I should've said was: "You know what, Chloe? This is mine. I did a really dumb thing that's kind of embarrassing. I wrote these notes and I tied them to balloon strings . . . and you don't need to know the details. Anyway, this is a note I wrote about a boy. I can't tell you who, but it doesn't matter anyway because of Fabio and all."

Instead, what I said was: "Wow. This is a major love note to you from Tao. I guess he's totally into you, just like you said."

"Ha! Told you!" Chloe said in Jess's face, then she went leaping back out into the hallway.

Jess scoffed. "Are you kidding, Abby? There's no way Tao sent a love note to Chloe."

I hated that I was throwing Tao under the bus. Tao, who was an all-around great guy, nice to everyone, cute, and good at math. He didn't deserve this. And Paige, my co-best friend? I'd never jeopardize our relationship to save myself from public humiliation, but here I was with uncontrollable diarrhea of the mouth again. Really, what I was doing was stalling for time. I needed to put fractions and factorials aside for some good old-fashioned detective work.

I told Jess, "But it's right there, in black and white in lovely calligraphy that his mom or sister probably helped him with."

"Well, I don't believe it," Jess said. "Just wait until Paige hears. She'll get to the bottom of this."

"Jess, with the arch snafu and dance pressures, I don't think Paige can be distracted right now. Maybe we shouldn't tell her."

"Good point," Jess said. "I'll talk to Tao. You hold down the fort here." She made it as far as the door but stopped like a dog hitting an electric fence. "Ugh. No hall pass."

Just then the school intercom blared, "Abby Gray, please report to the office."

"Good timing," I said. Having your name called over the intercom was the only way to get through the halls without a pass, unless you were Logan, who apparently had some superpower. "You know what? I have an idea. I'll catch Tao on my way to the office, and *I'll* ask him about it. Easiest, peasiest way to get to the bottom of this silly misunderstanding. I mean, there has to be some totally reasonable explanation. I bet this is just some mixed-up messages."

"Of course. Sounds good," Jess said. "Besides, I'm better at the color coordinating that needs to go on here." She paused. "Just sayin'."

You can see how she could sound mean, but she *was* better with a color wheel and matching patterns than I was. Except everything here was red and white—*how hard could it be?*

CHAPTER 7

The school office was total chaos. Principal Rashed spoke into the phone with a finger in his ear while a trio of sixth graders covered in mud sat in the "uh-oh chairs" waiting to see him. The office lady was literally buried under a mountain of red and white balloons, and from the sounds of grumbling, she wasn't happy about it.

"Hey, you," I said to Manny, student council president, who sorted through the council's suggestion box, mostly pulling out candy wrappers.

"Hi, Abs," he said.

Off to the side, Miss Young spoke to Mr. Valdez in hushed tones. Mr. Valdez was not only my math teacher but also the faculty sponsor of the Peppermint Twist dance. It looked like a serious conversation. I strained to eavesdrop while tilting my head at a poster about the school's social media policy.

I heard Mr. Valdez say, "I think it was her."

Miss Young asked, "What makes you think that?"

"Because I found it and not two seconds later, there she was, all smiles. It was her, I'm telling you. I'm eighty-nine percent sure." That was Mr. Valdez, always about numbers. Only his glasses and hair in need of a cut looked math teacher-y. The rest of him was dark straight-leg jeans and button-up Vineyard Vines tucked in neatly with no gut to hide. Outside of this building he could pass for a regular non-math-teacher guy. Unless he made one of his algebra jokes that only I thought were funny.

"Have you ever heard of a coincidence?" Miss Young asked, pulling her windblown locks into a low ponytail. She was pretty and perky in a former-cheerleader-turned-motorcycle-rider way. It was like her outside said one thing—girl next door. But inside, she wanted wind whipping her in the face and the rush of speed-induced adrenaline—badass. Weird combo, but it worked for her.

"Shouldn't I at least check it out?" he asked.

"No. You shouldn't. There is an unwritten teacher's oath. Maybe you've heard of it. It's called 'Teachers Don't Date Parents.'"

Dating parents? This was getting good. I wrinkled my brow with great interest in the fine print about cyberbullying and stepped a few inches closer.

"Geez. No one's *dating*. There's no *date*. I was just going to ask her. You know, to check. For clarity," Mr. Valdez said.

"Wouldn't want to be unclear."

"Exactly."

"Who are you trying to convince, Valdez, me or you?"

"I don't need to convince you. I'm a romantic, an old soul. There aren't many of us left. If I want to check this out in the name of romance, then maybe I will."

Oh, I totally got where he was coming from, only he was brave and I was a chicken who just wrote stupid notes, folded them up like stupid origami frogs, tied them to stupid strings, and let them float away on stupid red balloons. I mean, come on, Abby, *really*?

"You've already made up your mind." Miss Young put her mail in her motorcycle helmet and headed out, saying over her shoulder, "So go for it. You don't need my permission."

"No, I don't, and I'm gonna," Mr. Valdez said to her back. Then he looked around to see who'd heard him. He forced a smile when he saw me standing nearby. "Abby, hi there. Sorry to pull you out of the gym, but vans from the party store have been delivering balloons all morning." He indicated the office lady—well, her brown orthopedic shoes, since that was all we could see. "We gotta get them out of here before someone is smothered."

"I know. I already brought some to the gym." I looked around the office. "This room is about twenty by twenty, so four hundred square feet. Our balloons are about one cubic foot each, so a hundred of them would cover the ceiling. And we're expecting a thousand . . ."

"Which won't fit in here," he finished my thought.

"They were supposed to come with a guy who'd build them into the shape of an arch for over the gym door."

He glanced again at the shoes. "Well, someone messed up. We gotta get these to the gym faster than the speed of light—"

"Two hundred ninety-nine million seven hundred ninety-two thousand four hundred fifty-eight meters per second."

He smiled at my precision. "If we don't, we might have to call the paramedics. I don't want blood on my hands."

Principal Rashed slammed the phone into its cradle. "Valdez!" His voice was deep and totally scary.

"I'm right here," Mr. Valdez called over or around or through the mound of biodegradable latex.

Mr. Rashed punched a few balloons out of his way so he could see us. His bald, dark head glistened with sweat. "That was the superintendent on the phone. She just got an expense statement from Karleigh's Party Emporium that was authorized by one Paige Bakenya, chairwoman of The Mount Lebanon Middle School's Decoration Committee, of which I'm told you're the sponsor." His voice bellowed like a bullhorn, and if he were a cartoon, plumes of white-hot smoke would shoot out of his ears. "I didn't even know we had any such committee."

"We do," Mr. Valdez said.

"And Miss Bakenya has authority to spend fourteen hundred dollars on dance decorations?"

"Yes. That's the budget. Teaches the students responsibility."

"The superintendent seems to think that's a bit exorbitant, especially when we don't have funds to pay for new tongue depressors for the nurse. We make her wash the old ones and use them again, which is probably some kind of health code violation." He rubbed a handkerchief over his bald head. "Do you get my point?"

"Yes, I sure do," Mr. Valdez said.

"Abby Gray, aren't you also on that committee?"

"Yes, sir. I am. The thing is that the stuff is already bought. A lot of it is already hung up or painted. Or, well, in this room filled with helium."

Mr. Rashed sighed. "Well, now the superintendent is coming to the dance tonight, so these decorations had better be off-the-charts fantastic. I told her it was part of a graded pop art project that was important for fine art appreciation. I just wanted her to stop yelling at me. I don't like it when she calls to yell at me. I don't even know what pop art is, but your committee better create it by tonight."

"Yes, sir. If anyone can make that happen, Paige can." I believed that, but it was a lot of work for three girls to do in one day.

"I hope so, for your sake, because if the superintendent is not convinced, she said the decoration committee can reimburse the school for, and I quote, 'the outrageous expense it incurred.'" Principal Rashed waved the waiting, muddy kids into his office. "I don't think either of us wants that to happen, so please tell Paige Bakenya to make this all just go away." He pushed his door shut with a bang, then opened it again. "And get those balloons out of here!" Another slam.

I met eyes with Mr. Valdez and smiled nervously. This was a lot of pressure.

He turned to address Manny. "Do you think you can help the decoration committee out today?"

Manny was always up for helping. For as long as I could remember, he'd helped me with anything I needed. Sometimes I didn't even need to ask—he just knew. Like at the third-grade Field Day tug-of-war when I was so close to getting pulled into a mud pit, and he took the rope from me and splatted into the puddle in my place.

I didn't hear Manny's answer because of the girls I saw through the office window. They giggled over a folded piece of paper that I recognized.

Another note had dropped and been found.

Which one was it?

Then Logan entered the office. He gingerly lifted balloons to reveal a corner of the office lady's desk and slid pink memo slips underneath. They were snatched away by a hand attached to an unseen arm.

Mr. Valdez said to him, "Logan, put your deliveries on hold. I need you to help Abby and crew get the gym ready for the dance. The superintendent is coming."

"And I guess that's a big deal?"

"Huge," Mr. Valdez confirmed with a nod.

"I wouldn't go to class?"

"Correct."

"I'm in."

My phone buzzed in my pocket. I glanced at the photo that had just posted on InstaPic.

I could see the office window behind the picture. The girls in the hallway had just posted it along with "Discovered outside the Donut Hole on the way to school: a string tangled around a light post, a deflated balloon on one end, this note on the other."

The Hole was right next door to school.

The picture was of a note that said:

I lied to my friends.

9:00am

CHAPTER 8

Weak knees
  Sweating palms
    Ants in my pants

I had to do something about all of this.

Now.

"Um, do you guys think you could take these to the gym?" I asked Manny and Logan about the balloons. "I sort of have something I have to take care of."

I had to go out on a search.

"Not now, Abby. Your priority is that gym. You heard Principal Rashed," Mr. Valdez said. "Have you ever met the superintendent?"

"No."

"Neither have I, but I hear she's like the Incredible Hulk."

"Green?" Logan asked.

"No," Mr. Valdez said. "You wouldn't like her when she's angry."

"Huh?" I asked.

Manny explained. "You know, the guy is regular until he gets angry and then—"

Mr. Valdez interrupted and pointed to his watch. "Maybe you can sort this out while you're decorating."

"But," I said, my heart racing, "I have this conflict—"

He held up his hand. "Whatever it is, it can wait."

"But—" I tried one last time, only to get more of his hand.

Manny, Logan, and I loaded ourselves up with the balloons that entombed the office lady and carefully navigated them through the office door. Clearly, we had to make more trips before she was dug out enough to write detention slips.

"Oh, and Abby," Mr. Valdez called after me, "I just wrote a memo for you." He combed through a stack of paper he held in his arms. "I can't find it right now. I'll send someone to the gym with it when I get my hands on it. Be on the lookout."

"Okay." I figured he was sending me a certificate for mathematics excellence. I got those a lot. Little did he know about my grave miscalculation that could alter my middle-school existence. Maybe it was the altitude.

As I walked down the hall with the boys, I looked into a classroom and watched kids put their heads together and whisper.

Did they know it was me?

How could they know?

From those two notes, there was no way they could know. I was so glad I'd opted for calligraphy. They were probably saying something about me being with Logan and Manny. "Which one of them do you think she likes?" There was always talk like that at The Mount.

Manny pulled his phone out of his back pocket. "Ha! Very funny," he said.

"What is it?"

"The note about 'lying to my friends' that some seventh-grade girls found and posted on InstaPic. It's getting comments."

"Really?" I asked, super casually. "Like what?"

"Speculation about who wrote it," Manny said.

Before I could ask who was speculating what about who, Logan saw Ben (Jess's boyfriend) down the hall from us. "Yo, Benny!"

"What's with the balloons, dude?" Ben asked.

Logan handed his fistful of balloons to me. "Here, take these."

My hands were full. "Um . . . how am I going to do that?"

He looked at me and decided to tie them through the belt loop on the back of my jeans. There I was with Logan's hands just a few inches from my butt. I was wearing Lucky Brand jeans that I thought made it look good. If Logan thought so, he made no indication. "I'll catch up with you guys later." He ran ahead to meet Ben.

Manny said, "That's about the kind of help I expected from Logan."

"You know what?" I said when we reached a girls' restroom. "I need to stop here." I tied my balloon ribbons to the doorknob and untied the ribbons from my belt loop and tied them to the water fountain. "I'll meet you in the gym." And I dashed inside, leaving Manny in the hall.

A quick scan of the restroom told me I was alone. I looked in the mirror and talked to myself. "You've made one heck of a mess. You will never write a note and tie it to a balloon and let it fly away ever again. *Never.*" I looked at my reflection. "Think, think. Okay, if you can find out exactly where those balloons fell, you can use that variable to construct an equation to calculate where the others will fall. Then you can intercept them, and this problem will be solved before anyone knows about your crush . . . before anyone knows—"

Then it happened:

The toilet flushed.

My cheeks flushed.

Someone was in the restroom. Someone had heard me.

Could this day get any worse?

No Regrets Ceremony? How dumb could I be?

Under the stall I saw black Doc Martens hit the ground. I knew who was attached to them. She came out of the stall with a big-daddy grin on her braced face.

This day *had* just gotten worse—a lot worse.

CHAPTER 9

It was Nikki White, otherwise known as Shadow. Not because kids called her Shadow, but because she called *herself* Shadow, and she kept invisible pugs in her pockets. Seriously, she pretended that little dogs lived in her pockets.

"Hey there, Shadow. What's up?"

"A lot, I think." I could tell she'd heard every word. "You're in a jam, aren't you, Abby Gray?"

"I don't know what you mean."

"Give it up. I saw Chloe this morning, so I know exactly what's going on. I might not be the smart girl, but I ain't stupid. I bet you want my help."

I didn't. "Do you know how I can fix this?"

"Heck, no." Shadow's braces were so complex they made her cheeks puff out. Her hair was poodle-curly. "But I know what *I'm* gonna do about it."

"What?" I hoped she wasn't going to tell anyone.

"I'm gonna tell everyone!"

Right there in the girls' restroom, my world imploded. If I'd had to pee, I'd have wet my pants.

I had to calm down, but how could I when I was insanely close to being the outcast? *I'd* be the new Shadow of the school.

> ***I could've said:*** "Oh, please don't. I'll do anything. I'll be your best friend. Whatever it takes. But please don't tell anyone. You have no idea how bad this could get for me."
>
> ***And what I said was:*** "Big whoop. Whatev."

I washed my hands and left the girls' restroom only to turn right back around, go back in, and say, "Oh, Nikki, please don't."

She growled at me for calling her Nikki. (She did that sometimes.)

"Sorry, I mean *Shadow*, please don't."

"I don't see how I have any other choice," she said. "This is just the chance I've been waiting for. If everyone is laughing at you, they'll leave me alone. It's my lucky day." Then she made a baby-talk voice and said into her pocket, "Isn't it my lucky day?" She barked like a ventriloquist so it would seem like the sound was coming out of her pocket—the pretend pugs agreeing with her.

Shadow was right. She was the one the kids mocked. In their defense, when you called yourself Shadow and talked to annoying little invisible dogs and made a make-believe doghouse in the schoolyard and barked at people when they walked by, there was a lot of material to work with. If the attention was focused on me, she'd get a break.

"Unless . . . ," she said.

"Yeah?"

"There could be a way."

"Name it," I said.

And she did.

It wasn't good.

10:00am

CHAPTER 10

I walked into the gym to find that Chloe had returned, but Paige hadn't. Chloe beamed as she talked to Jess, who was trying to hang streamers. It didn't seem like Chloe or Jess had seen the latest on InstaPic yet.

Manny sat on the bleachers, entertained by their exchange.

"I already told you. I don't think you two make a good couple," Jess said to Chloe as she worked on the wall. "For starters, he has a girlfriend."

"Tsk." Chloe propped her hands on her hips.

"Just sayin'." Jess shrugged.

Chloe seemed to accept this as an apology, but as someone close to the source, I knew Jess didn't mean it as one. She quoted my note: "'*My heart aches* . . .' It's so classic, isn't it? I can't wait until the dance. Everyone will see Tao and me together."

"Any luck clearing this up?" Jess asked me.

"No. I got sidetracked by pop art, orthopedic shoes, tongue depressors, the Hulk—"

The gym door opened with a *bang* as it slammed against the wall. Shadow entered with more balloons than I ever could've carried in one trip.

I finished, "And pugs."

"The office lady has been set free," Shadow announced, "thanks to yours truly and her four-legged team."

Chloe said, "Someone let the dogs out. That's my cue to leave." She waltzed out of the gym and then back in again. "I almost forgot. This is for you." Chloe threw an official teacher message—not the kind for academic excellence, the kind students get when they're in trouble—on the ground near our feet. Then she danced away without telling us who it was for.

Jess opened it and read out loud:

MOUNT LEBANON MIDDLE SCHOOL
MEMO

Dear Student,
Your teacher requests a parent meeting.
TIME: 3:00 PM
PLACE: Coffee Station
FROM: Mr. Valdez

Jess dropped it on the floor. "Not it!" She threw her arms up in the air as if that would actually mean the note wasn't for her.

"It can't be for me. I got an A on yesterday's test," I said.

"Minus," Jess said. "You told me you got an A-*minus*. It's not the same thing. You're capable of A-pluses."

Geez, I'd gotten an A-minus because Mr. Valdez gave me extra questions, high-school-level trig. I'd gotten just a small part of one of the questions wrong, so Mr. Valdez gave me an A-minus knowing that would make me try harder.

Jess added, "Plus you're always daydreaming and stuff. The rest of us pay attention. I'm just sayin', maybe you're not as smart as you used to be."

"You have a D in math!"

"But I'm working to my *po-ten-tial*," Jess said.

Shadow interrupted. "It's not for us." She used the plural to include the pugs. "My dad just left from a morning parent-teacher meeting." She looked over at Manny, who was opening boxes of decorations. "You?"

"I've never gotten one of those memos, and I don't think today is any different." He ripped open another box.

Jess said, "Well, I'm not telling my mom to go to *your* parent-teacher conference." She refolded the memo and snapped it out for me to take, and in doing so revealed the "To" on the outside.

"Ha!" She pointed to my name. "See! It really is for you."

"Fine!" I took the memo and shoved it in my back pocket. Of course, give the parent-teacher conference to the kid having the

WORST
DAY
OF
HER
LIFE!

Could I really be in trouble for something?

Then I thought some more about the conversation I'd overheard in the office. Could my mom be the parent he wanted to date?

Mr. Valdez was a nice guy and everything, and my mom was great. She worked long hours in a lab, which was okay, because I could take care of myself, and finding a cure for cancer was awfully important work, especially to us, because my dad died from cancer when I was four. I planned to do the same kind of work, but I also wanted to fly to the moon (or Mars), teach gorillas sign language, and invent something that could suck pollution out of the air, if someone didn't beat me to it. But my mom dating a teacher from my school?

What if they were seen together and someone posted it on InstaPic?

What would the other kids think?

What would they say?

I texted my mom about the parent-teacher meeting, its time and location. She instantly replied, "Ok."

Shadow tied the mass of balloons onto a few chairs and walked around the gym like an inspector. She picked a peppermint stick candy out of a box and made a noisy act of unwrapping the cellophane and sucking. She took a second stick, broke it in two, and dropped each half into a pocket. Neither Jess nor I had to ask why.

Jess said, "Thanks for the balloons. You can be on your merry little way now."

"I'm gonna hang out," she said. "In here. With *you*. And help you cats out." At the mention of cats, she acted as though there was a flurry of activity from her pockets.

I prayed that Jess and Paige would be okay with this. Maybe they'd even be happy that I'd rounded up some extra help.

Shadow whispered into her pocket, "It's okay."

Paige returned to the gym with printed directions, wire, and clippers. She'd heard Shadow. "I'm the chairwoman of this committee, and I say who can help and who can't."

"Is that so?" Shadow asked. "Because if I can't help, I'm sure I could make myself busy sharing some juicy news I just heard."

Jess perked up. "Oooohhh. What?"

CHAPTER 11

"Hey!" I clapped to get the girls' attention. "Let's focus. We have a dance to dazzle. Lots to do. Last time I looked at that door right there, I didn't see a balloon arch. We really need the extra help, so I'm really appreciative that Shadow offered to pitch in when I saw her in the restroom. I told her it was okay." I gave Jess and Paige a *this is a no-brainer* look, which wasn't easy because I felt like *she's blackmailing me, I'm desperate, so please just be okay with this.* "It is okay, isn't it? We need her more than you know." I explained what Mr. Rashed had told me about the superintendent, expenses, reimbursement, and pop art.

Paige stood with her perfect posture (back straight, shoulders back), purple feathery pen in hand, and studied her planner. "I live for pressure. Maybe she can decorate the stage." She looked toward the stage and saw Manny sitting on the bleachers. He'd grabbed a bag of chips from one of the boxes, opened it, and popped them into his mouth like they were movie theater popcorn and we were the movie.

"What's he doing here?" Paige asked.

"Oh," I said. "Good news. Principal Rashed, in a panic over the phone call from the superintendent, sent reinforcements. Logan's around somewhere too."

"Why is our reinforcement eating our refreshments?" Jess asked.

"I'll talk to him about that," I said, "and get him started on something easy—you know, something he can't mess up."

Paige puffed out a huge sigh. "Sweeping would be good."

"Good idea." I called to Manny, "Could you sweep?"

"Aye-aye, captain," he said.

Then to everyone else I said, "Let's get to work, people."

Jess went back to her stripes.

I walked over to Manny and took the chips. "These

are for tonight." I rolled the bag shut and put it back in the box.

"Watching those girls is like reality TV. I like to crunch on stuff when I watch TV," he said.

"We're behind schedule here. Paige doesn't like being behind schedule. Principal Rashed is breathing down our necks, the school has a shortage of tongue depressors, and we have no arch maker."

"Don't forget about random notes popping up." He chuckled.

How could I forget? I blushed and he stared at me, which made me blush more.

"What?" I asked, and instinctively wiped my nose like maybe he'd seen a booger.

"What's wrong?" he asked.

"Nothing. There's just a lot going on after sweeping. Can you move those boxes over there and start unfolding tables and chairs?" I asked.

"Sure, Abs. Whatever you need." That was so Manny. He was always helping me, and he always let me have my way. We made our own Power Ranger costumes for Halloween one time. He wanted to be Teenage Mutant Ninja Turtles, but I wanted to be Power

Rangers. And for some reason I insisted he should be the pink one. So he was a pink Power Ranger, even though I knew he really wanted to be Michelangelo.

Next I showed Shadow the big cardboard cut-out hearts. Keeping her busy seemed like a good way to keep her mind off spilling my beans. "These need to be taped all along the edge of the stage. Got it?"

"Yup. But what else? What else are you gonna do to get me included as one of your pack? Remember our deal?"

"We aren't a pack. We're a decoration committee. You're here. You're decorating. It's a start. I'm not a magician. Just be cool and blend in. That might help."

She taped a heart onto the edge of the stage. It was perfect. If she kept this up, maybe Paige would let her stay. She asked me, "You mean I should act like someone I'm not?"

> ***What I should've said was:*** "Of course not. You should always be yourself. People who matter will like you just the way you are."
> ***But instead, what I said was:*** "*Yes*! That's exactly what I mean."

She stopped taping.

"What?" I asked. "Is there a problem?"

"No problem, but I have an idea." She reached into her pocket, and I was pretty sure she was going to take out a pug. She didn't. She had two silver-studded black collars. She put one on. "Instead of me acting like everyone else to fit in, maybe if some of the popular kids started acting more like me, I could fit in." She handed me the collar.

"I'm not wearing this," I said, although I loved that she referred to me as one of the popular kids.

She reached for a microphone that was lying on the stage. "Are you sure?" Shadow flipped the switch on the mic. "Is this thing on?"

Shadow's voice bellowed through the gym and into the hall.

Paige barked, "Don't play with that."

Just then I had a thought. To Shadow I said, "Look. Even if the last note falls—"

"I'm guessing that one's about your crush that you *think* is secret. But I see things, Abby. I know who it is."

Just when I thought things couldn't get worse. Shadow had even more dirt on me. I said, "Even if that note falls and is found, and you tell people it's me, they won't believe you. I have a boyfriend."

"Funny thing about that . . ." Shadow smiled, showing thousands of dollars of orthodontics.

CHAPTER 12

Shadow said, "I did a little research. Seems there's no one named Fabio Risotto in the town of Christmas, Maine." She paused for a sec. "And really, Abby, *Risotto*? What a dumb name."

I'd come up with it on the fly, and I guessed it was a little dumb. "It's not dumb," I said. "And how would you know that?"

"Well, you don't have to be Nancy Drew to call the only middle school in Christmas and chat up the part-time secretary. You're not going to believe this—she has pugs! So, to help a fellow pug lover, she checked the school's records. No Fabio Risotto there. Ever."

Unbelievable.

What kind of a dork makes up a boyfriend?

If Shadow blabbed about this, I might be able to brush it off that she was the one making stuff up. That is, if I hadn't also written a note confessing that I'd made up a boyfriend.

I mean, who does that? And by "that" I mean:

Number one: Who makes up a boyfriend?
And number two: Who confesses it in a note that they let float away on a balloon string?

"What's it gonna be?" Shadow asked, holding up the collar.

I hesitated.

She tapped the mic again.

The *pat pat* vibrated off the glazed gym floor and right through my gut.

Paige snapped her manicured fingers without looking up from her planner.

Shadow turned the mic off. "I was just checking it," she called over to Paige. "Well?" she asked me.

I put the black studded dog collar around my neck.

"It looks great on you," she whispered.

"Just tape the stage." I squinted my eyes and narrowed my lips at her. How ruthless. "I have some things I have to take care of."

I returned to the other side of the gym, where Paige and Jess carefully studied the arch-making directions, to tell them I needed to go to the nurse.

When Jess glanced up, she saw the collar. "Oh dear gods of fashion. In the name of Michael Kors, what are you wearing?"

"What?" I asked. "Oh, this? Shadow gave it to me. I like it," I lied. "It's all the rage in Paris, I think."

Jess said, "I know what's all the rage in Paris. And that's not it."

Paige ignored the fashion talk completely. "We're going to tie the ribbons to the wire like this." She took a ribbon and demonstrated.

Jess did one.

"That looks good," I said. "I'll be right back. All this pressure is getting to me. I think I need to go to the nurse. Get an aspirin." But what I really needed was to find out exactly where Tao found that balloon so I could create an equation and get the other notes before anyone else. I was also curious why he'd give the note to Chloe. Could he actually like her?

"Oh, get a grip, Abby," Paige said. "You can't run off to the nurse when things get tough. And we can't afford to lose a key member of the decoration committee right now. We need you to tie ribbons to the wire."

Jess added, "You know, I heard she reuses the tongue depressors."

I sighed and tied.

We all tied quietly for a few minutes, then Paige said, "While I was printing these directions, I heard some kids say that Mr. Valdez is crushing on a parent."

Jess inhaled a quick, sharp, excited breath and said, "Shut the shop door!"

"Front door," I corrected her.

"That's totally 1990s. I'm making it 'shop door,' because starting trends is what I do."

Maybe I could make dog collars a trend.

"Abby, I bet Valdez is crushing on your mom. That's why he wants to meet her," Jess said.

"No. That was about my grade. Remember, you said I wasn't working to my potential," I said, but I was thinking about how Mr. Valdez looked at my mom this morning, and maybe Jess was right.

"I just made up that shop door before I knew the

memo was really for you," she said. "I mean, a parent-teacher conference at the Coffee Station? It's totally a date."

"Do you think Mr. Valdez is hot for your mom?" Paige asked. "I mean, why wouldn't he be? She's cute, single . . ."

Lots of kids at school had single parents, but Jess and Paige weren't among them.

Paige's mom and dad carpooled to work at the TV station, where her dad was the weatherman and her mom did the traffic report. Mrs. and Mr. Bakenya were a power couple if there ever was one.

Jess's mom worked for a big international company and traveled all over the world. Often her dad joined her, and they posted picture-perfect moments on social media. While Mr. and Mrs. Sawyer traveled, Jess and her three older sisters were free to shop online. They had enough shoes to supply a village.

"Don't worry," Jess said. "We won't tell anyone. No one will know."

"No one will know" was a total and complete impossibility at The Mount. It was a feat attempted but never achieved. News spread like bedbugs in a recycled mattress warehouse.

❤ ❤ ❤

Tying the strings was slow and tedious.

"This is going to take longer than I'd scheduled." Paige glanced over to make sure Shadow was doing an acceptable job with the stage, then asked, "So, what else is new?"

Jess said, "Oh, you'll never believe this. Chloe came in before—"

I took a balloon and, as casually as possible, squeezed it super hard right next to Jess's ear.

POP!

Both girls yelped.

"What the heck, Abby?" Jess asked.

"Accident, sorry. You okay?"

She rubbed her ear. I bent in close and whispered, "Remember, we weren't going to tell Paige."

She nodded. "Sure. Although I'm not great at keeping secrets."

No, duh.

Paige asked, "What are you two whispering about?"

"Nothing," I said.

"Yup. Nothing," Jess said. "Nothing at all. Nothing about Chloe and—"

POP!

They yelped again.

> ***What I wanted to say was:*** "Just keep your kisser closed long enough for me to fix this mess, starting with Tao, which is where I'm going right now. Cover for me while I make a run for it."
>
> ***Instead, what I said was:*** "Glitter!"

Paige's entire face lit up at the word.

"We need lots of glitter to sprinkle on this balloon arch. It will glisten like . . . like a . . . like a magical fairy-tale dream. I'll go get it."

Paige said, "*Yes*! You're a genius, Abby. *I'll* get glitter, and you gals can start on the flowers." And she flew out the door with the hall pass.

I'd learned all about glitter when I made the cute basket of assorted items for Paige for Christmas last year. She loved it. And she'd made me math symbol wall adhesives (%, ÷, √, ±, ≠) for my bedroom in colors that matched my comforter.

Jess and I divided up the bucket of red and white carnations into vases and put them on round tables that Manny had unfolded and set up against the wall according to the diagram Paige had drawn.

Shadow was more than halfway done with the stage, and it looked great. Not kidding.

"Hey." Manny interrupted my thoughts.

I looked up.

"Are you okay?"

"Okay? Sure. I'm okay. Great. It's gonna be a great day. And night. A great dance. I love dances, don't you?" I couldn't wait for this day to end.

Manny studied me and said, "You sound totally okay."

"Well, okay then."

"Yeah?" he confirmed, not believing that all this was, in fact, okay.

Manny knew me so well. He could probably see right through me.

I couldn't tell him about my biggest whammy of the day, which wasn't the only thing bugging me, so I said, "Um. You see, I think Mr. Valdez might like my mom."

"That's cool."

"You think?" I asked him.

"It doesn't matter what I think," he said. "What do you think?"

I didn't answer him, because I didn't know what I thought. I was more worried about what Jess and Paige would think. But now that I thought about it, maybe it wasn't such a big deal.

"I think I need to fix these." I reorganized the carnations so each vase had two red and two white. I needed even numbers right now.

"And what's the deal with Chloe, Shadow, and the balloon popping?" Manny asked.

"You caught all that?"

"I'm pretty observant," Manny said. "Uh, and . . ." He pointed to his neck. "The dog collar? That's hard to miss."

I looked into his familiar, friendly eyes and considered telling him about the notes. It would be nice to have someone on my side.

"I haven't seen you act this weird since third grade, when you gave cake to Chloe's pet turtle at her birthday party and it died."

"Shh," I said. "You have no idea how terrible I feel about that to this day. And she still doesn't know. You're the only one I ever told."

"And I've kept *that* secret, so tell me what's going on now."

Jess brought red and white tablecloths over to me and Manny and said, "I figured it out. Abby, I know what's going on."

11:00am

CHAPTER 13

That's it.

I was done.

Jess knew I wrote the two notes, which weren't horrible, but she didn't know how much worse this could get.

My new life would be "ShadowPugsAndAbby."

"You do?" I asked, then held my breath.

"Yup. Chloe wrote that note to herself, and she's telling everyone that it's from Tao. I mean, come on, did you read that mushy crap? Who does that?"

> ***What I should've said was:*** "No, that's not it. I wrote that mushy crap, Jess. If I knew people were going to see it, I would've done a better job. Keeping my crush a secret was killing me.

And I lied about Fabio, the concert, and the boots, and, Jess, there's something else big I've lied about."

But instead, what I said was: "Yeah. You're probably right. It's just the sort of thing she would do. If for no other reason, just to upset Paige."

"Too right, Abby."

Just then Nosepicker Gordon came in the gym. "Uh, hi. I have this book for Paige."

"I'm right here, Gord." Paige walked in behind him, as if on cue. "With *glitter*!" Her arms were full. She let the containers fall onto a table and hit her back pocket. "Oh crap. I dropped the hall pass somewhere."

Gordon said, "That's as good as gone-zo."

"Ugh," she said.

He handed her a science book. "This is from Ben."

"Ben?" Jess jumped in. "He probably meant for you to give it to *me*."

"It's for me," Paige said. "I'm borrowing it because mine had some pages ripped out."

"Oh, all right then," Jess said.

"RReeeow!" Shadow made a sound like a cat fighting in response to Paige and Jess bickering about the science book.

"Mind your own business," Jess called over to her.

Gordon looked around. "The place looks good." He spit when he talked.

Gordon was the type of guy who patiently waited for a growth spurt and the day his freckles would start fading. He rubbed his bony elbow and winced.

"You hurt yourself?" Shadow called across the gym.

"Chloe hip-checked me into a locker earlier. She was dancing all crazy around the science wing." He tried to lift his arm up to see the underside of it. "Is there a bruise?"

Paige said, "Chloe Chloe Chloe. That's all I've heard today. Why is everyone talking about her today?"

> ***What I should have said was:*** "She got a love note. She thinks it's from Tao. But don't worry, it's not. Tao totally likes you. And funny story actually, but I wrote that note. It's not really important who I was writing it to, but Shadow found out, and she's threatening to tell everyone if I don't get her in our pack—that's her word,

not mine. So, let's just let her in the pack, and we can put this all behind us. Sound good?"

Instead, I said: "Are we gonna curl those ribbons and hang them? They are the shop door. I love them."

"Good one," Jess said, referring to my "shop door" comment.

"Maybe over there?" I suggested, indicating the side of the gym farthest from the arch. "That will make the far side of the room equally as fab as this side."

"Very true," Paige called. "Your eye for *feng shui* is getting better since we've been working on it."

We had been working on it. We binge-watched a whole season of *Interesting Interiors* one night, and the next day we went to a TEDx Talk about the history of square roots. I loved it. The TEDx, that is. Actually, *Interesting Interi*ors wasn't bad either, and I learned about color distribution.

"Hey, Gordon," I said. "How are you at curling ribbon?"

"Uh—I—uh—I don't like to brag, but I've been known to—"

"You're hired," I said.

"Not so fast," Paige said. "He'll need to audition." She demonstrated how to run the sharp blade over the ribbon.

Gordon took the scissors and ribbon. His tryout yielded a scraped thumb and a mediocre curl.

"Let's try again," Paige said. "Your tiny hands should be good for this." She launched into an animated, one-on-one tutorial that successfully distracted everyone from talking about Chloe. And guess what? Gordon's ribbons were amazing—tight Qs worthy of Paige's approval.

Manny tugged my shirt and pulled me aside. "Okay. Enough. Now spill it."

"Chloe got a love note from Tao."

"Everyone knows that," he said.

"Everyone except Paige," I corrected. "But what everyone doesn't know is that it's not really from Tao. He didn't write it."

That's when Ben's science book caught my eye. Well, not the book, but the corner of a paper sticking out of the book.

"Hang on," I said to Manny.

I recognized these creases. If folded along them, the paper would make a perfect origami frog.

I walked over to it. "Can I see that?" I asked Paige.

Paige asked, "The book?"

"Yeah."

"Abby, this is no time for mitosis. We have way too much work to do."

"Just for a sec," I said.

She handed me the book. "Manny is doing well. I mean, he's no Gordon, but he has potential."

I hardly heard the comment. I faked opening to the table of contents while I slid the folded paper out and casually tucked it into my sleeve.

"What's that?" Paige asked and snatched it before I had completely hidden it.

"Probably trash." I tried to get it from her.

She moved it out of my reach. "It's a note." With a mischievous tone she said, "I wonder what it says."

CHAPTER 14

I was sweating. "If you don't recognize it, then it's not yours. And you know, it's kinda rude to take someone's personal note like that and read it."

She ignored me, read it to herself, and mumbled, "*My heart aches to be so much in love and not be able to tell you or anyone . . .*"

She lowered her voice and said to me, "Ben sent me a love note in his science book. Why would he do that?" Then she whispered, "You think maybe Ben likes me?"

I couldn't respond, because I couldn't catch my breath.

How much more confusion could that one little piece of paper cause?

What neither Paige nor I knew was that Jess had walked up behind us.

"Well, that's just great," she said, her eyes filled with tears. "Do you like him too?"

Paige said, "What? No. I would *never* have a thing for my best friend's boyfriend. That's the worst thing a friend could ever do."

"Oh, so true," Shadow said. She'd somehow gotten ridiculously close to us, worming her way into the pack. "That's the oldest love triangle in the book." She lowered her voice and confided in us, "Only in the book, usually someone gets murdered."

Paige's eyebrows lifted at the notion that Jess might kill her over Ben.

"That's what happens in the book," Shadow said.

There was a beat of silence that defined "awkward."

I swallowed hard. "Huh. I wonder if we have that book in the library. I—I—I'll go look for it." Ah, the perfect excuse to get out of here and pick up my stalled investigation.

Shadow said, "It's not *really* a book, Abby." I knew that, of course, but grasped for any excuse to hunt the halls. Then to Paige, Shadow said, "Looks like your best friend's boyfriend likes you."

Jess wiped her nose on a red napkin from the refreshment table. "Ben and me probably wouldn't have worked out anyway. I knew it was too good to be true."

> ***What Paige should've said was:*** "Everything will be fine. This is just a misunderstanding. Of course Ben likes you. Let's talk to him and figure this out."
> ***Instead, what she said was:*** "It's good you found out now before things got any more serious. If he kept his love for me a secret, there's no telling what else he could be hiding."

"Like what? You think he's hiding something else? How would you know that?" Jess was getting majorly agitated. "Has he told you some big secret?"

"Oh, no." While Paige remained calm, my pulse raced. Paige said, "I've never even talked to Ben about secrets. I was just saying that maybe you don't know him as well as you think you do."

"Really? Or maybe you're just trying to make me think he's got all these other secrets that he isn't telling me, so that I'll let him go, and you can have him all to yourself."

"I don't want him. I have a boyfriend who, by the way, is great friends with Ben," Paige said.

Gordon's hands wildly spiraled large quantities of ribbons. "We guys don't poach our friends' girlfriends," he said like a relationship expert. "It's not cool." He spat a little on the *c* in "cool."

> ***What Jess should have said was:*** "You're right, Gordon. Good point. You know a lot about this stuff. Ben would never do that. There's obviously been a mix-up."
>
> ***Instead, what Jess said was:*** "Too bad Tao likes Chloe."

"What?!" Paige cried.

Jess asked herself, "Did I just go there?"

Ugh. My arrhythmia was getting worse.

"Yup," Gordon answered. "You did." He swiped a scissor down a ribbon, making a bouncy curl.

Shadow laughed. "You totally did."

"What do you mean, Tao likes *Chloe*?" Paige asked.

"Everyone knows. He gave her a love note this morning," Jess said.

Paige's eyes got moist.

How could I let Paige be sad about this?

I gave Jess an *I thought we weren't going to tell her* look, and she said, "I know this is hard to hear and I'm really sorry. I don't want to hurt your feelings, but you have a right to know."

Paige sniffed.

To Paige I said, "Don't pay attention to her. The love note Tao gave Chloe was probably nothing. A misunderstanding."

Paige yelled at me, "You knew about *this*!" She smacked her hand on the table—the hand holding the love note she thought was from Ben—the same one Chloe thought was from Tao—and set the paper down.

"I never believed Tao really wrote it in the first place," I said through a dry mouth.

Shadow said, "Neither did I! In fact, I'm pretty confident about that."

I tilted my head at her. She wasn't helping.

When Paige wiped her eyes, I casually slid the note into my pocket, where it could be nice and safe until I found a garbage disposal, a Bunsen burner, or some decoupage. Then I was able to take a breath.

Jess and Paige continued loudly "discussing" the situation, with Gordon offering advice as they spoke. I saw this as an opportunity to investigate the discovery locations of the first two notes. I hoped to use those coordinates to predict the drop locations of the yet-un-discovered messages. My pulse started to steady. It was the perfect time for me to make a quiet exit and find Tao, the guy I figured would have info about the drop location of this morning's note.

I backpedaled toward the door, ready to bolt, when I realized there was a problem with my exit plan. There was only one person who could help me fix it—The King of Hall Passes.

Noon

CHAPTER 15

In response to my 911 text, Logan Murphy appeared, almost magically.

"That was fast. Weren't you in class?" I asked him.

"No," he said. "Remember, Mr. Valdez cleared my schedule all day so I could help with the dance prep?" He scanned the gym. "Looks good."

"Oh, gee, thanks. You've been a huge help."

"Well, I'll leave if you don't need me."

"Okay. Sorry, sorry. Yes, you've been a huge help today. Now, here's the deal. I need a hall pass to take care of something . . . something personal."

"Like a girl thing?"

"Not exactly. Maybe. Sort of. Can you help me?"

"Well, I'm not working in the office today because I'm here."

"Oh, I thought you were The Man, that you could move stealthily around the halls. I must've been mistaken."

That did it. He wasn't going to miss the opportunity to prove to me that he was The Man.

"Follow me," he said. "On the way, you can tell me what's going on."

"What do you mean? Nothing is going on."

He looked at the collar on my neck. "Right."

We walked for a minute without saying anything else, then he pulled me around the corner, slapped his palm over my mouth, and made a "shh" with his lips. I was sandwiched between his basketball jersey and the wall. I hadn't been this close to Logan since we played Twister at Jess's Halloween party. My besties made me an amazing calculator costume. Paige sewed each button, and Jess advised on the fabric colors. It was so good. Logan was dressed as a trash bag and had the smell to make the costume complete. Now he smelled like peppery soap and cinnamon gum. I liked it.

Just then, Principal Rashed passed through the main corridor, not seeing us where Logan had tucked us away.

"Follow me," he said when Rashed was gone. "Do exactly what I do."

I copied all of his Special Forces moves through the halls, including an army crawl on the floor under the library windows. He'd definitely done this before. We made it to the outside of the main office without getting spotted. He took out his cell phone and dialed.

While waiting for an answer, he asked, "Who are you going to the dance with? Your boyfriend?"

Before I could lie . . . er . . . answer, he put his index finger in front of his lips. Then, in a low voice, he said into the phone, "Hello. This is water delivery. I'm locked outside the cafeteria door."

The office lady said, "Oh, hi, Kevin. I'll be right there." She flew out the door, a fog of freshly sprayed perfume following her.

Logan stuck his foot in the door so the latch wouldn't catch. "She has the hots for the water dude." He slipped into the office and swiped two hall passes off the counter.

He held them up for me. "Presto," he said. "Do you have anything you want to say?"

"Thanks. You're The Man."

He smiled with great satisfaction.

I grabbed a pass and dashed away without answering the date question.

> ***The good news:*** That pass gave me flexibility, abilities, and the power to mill about the school to conduct my mission. I wasn't invisible, but I was one step closer to finding out where the first note fell and triangulating the most likely drop zone of the other notes. I watched snow accumulating outside. They were out there somewhere.
>
> ***The bad news:*** With or without a pass, I was stuck inside, putting the undiscovered notes just out of my reach.

I took off down the hallway.

"Hey," Logan called after me. "Where's the fire?" He caught up. "I'm coming too."

I didn't slow down. "Trust me, Logan. You don't want to be around me. I'm having kind of a really bad day." The breeze from my speed blew hair out of my face as I walked fast, with purpose, through one corridor, then the next.

"That's just the kind of cryptic info that makes me want to find out what you're up to."

"Go back to the gym," I said. "The decoration committee needs you."

"They'll be fine. They have Gordon. He's like a wizard with a glue gun. Why are you trying to get rid of me?"

I didn't answer. Each teacher I passed, I flashed the hall pass like FBI credentials giving me authority to inspect any area of the school I felt like entering, which it pretty much did. Logan had to jog to keep up.

Finally, he passed me and blocked me. I sidestepped, but he was too fast and blocked me again.

"Fine. You can tag along."

He got close to my face and said, "I was gonna anyway."

"Just don't get in my way. I mean it. I have a lot to do."

If I hadn't already had a crush, I could have maybe been into Logan Murphy, just like everyone else.

CHAPTER 16

Snow had transitioned from flurries to full, fluffy flakes.

I peeked in each classroom window as nonchalantly as I could, looking for Tao: in the art room, the computer lab, the music room. When we passed the library, I saw Ben, which meant Tao was probably nearby.

I marched in. The librarian was about to ask me what I was doing there, but I held up the pass and she let me enter. Ben was playing table hockey with Jeremy. "We need to talk," I said to him.

When he looked up at me, Jeremy scored.

"Not cool, Abby. This better be good."

"It is."

Ben was in eighth grade too, but he turned fifteen this year when everyone else was turning fourteen, because he'd done kindergarten twice. Since he'd been spending so much time at the skate park, he'd started looking different—a little older and skate-boardier.

"Do you know where Tao is?"

"Not sure. I wasn't assigned to watch him today."

Jeremy smiled at Ben's joke. "Good one, Benny."

I said to Jeremy, "Can this be . . . ummm . . . private?"

"I'm not going anywhere," he said. He was *the* class jerk.

I leaned into Logan's ear. "If you wanna help, get him outta here."

Logan said, "Hey, Jeremy, I hear you're into bugs. I saw a really hairy dude by the reference section. Wanna see it?"

"You know it!" Jeremy said, and followed Logan. "But hey, man, I can't hang with you for long. I've gotta cut outta this taco stand soon to get an allergy shot."

Once Logan and Jeremy were out of earshot, I said, "Sorry about the hockey game."

Ben eyed my neck and the collar. "What's with that?"

"Long, boring story. Never mind that. Look"—I took the note out of my jeans—"I only have one question for you. Where did this come from?" I paused. "And why did you give it to Paige?"

"That's two questions. I thought you were good at math, Abby Gray. You know what your problem is? You don't pay attention to details. Probably why you got that A-minus." He took the note and looked at it.

"How did you know about my math grade?"

"People talk," he said with a shrug. "To answer your first question: I got this from Chloe. She put it on my tray at lunch, next to my hoagie—"

"Lemme stop you right there," I said. "Hoagie?"

"It's hoagie day."

Hoagie day was my favorite of all cafeteria lunches. Not just me, everyone, and they were usually all gone by one o'clock. I really didn't want to miss my favorite lunch. I looked at the time—twelve thirty. I should be good. "Okay, continue—"

"Salami, ham, provolone—"

"I know what's on a hoagie." But the details made my mouth water. "Tell me about the note."

"Sure, but it was really good. I read it and assumed Chloe had the hots for me, which is understandable. But she should be aware that Jess beat her to this"—he indicated himself—"and we're a thing or something. But whatev—I get that she needed to express herself. Girls are like that with 'feelings' and everything. I have sisters. I know stuff."

Apparently, he didn't know that there's a fine line between confidence and arrogance, and Ben had just crossed it. Regardless, I got my answer.

I filtered out everything after "I got it from Chloe."

He continued, "Question number two: I didn't give it to Paige. I gave Paige my science book because hers had missing pages. I was *sharing.* That's the kind of considerate guy I am, which is probably why Chloe's in love with me." If I'd already eaten, I might've puked a hoagie. "If Chloe sent you to talk to me for her, tell her thanks, but I'm not interested. Now I've got a question for you, Abby."

"What?"

"Why do you have my private love note in your pocket? And why do you care?"

I didn't mention that was two questions. "This was in your science book that you loaned to Paige."

He nodded like he was just starting to understand, flipped open a three-ring binder, and wiggled his fingers into a side pocket, where he found a folded paper similar to the love note. He opened it. "That explains it."

"What?"

"My science notes are right here. The exact science notes that I meant to give to Paige. To *shaaaare* since she missed class because of one of her club meetings. This is what's referred to as a *switch-up*."

Out of nowhere, Chloe marched up to the table and whacked Ben on the shoulder.

"What was that for?" he asked. "Oh, I know, you're jealous because I'm talking to Abby. But she's just a friend, and I hate to break it to you like this, but there ain't going to be anything between us. Okay?"

"What are you talking about?" she asked.

"The fact that you have a little thing for me. Sorry, it's not gonna happen."

"I don't know what you've got going on between your ears, but I don't have the hots for you. Maybe you should wear a helmet when you skate. Newsflash. Me and Tao are like a thing, like an I-T-E-M," Chloe said. "But I'm here because you didn't meet me."

"Meet you where?"

"Did you forget that I asked you to meet me at the swings so you could give me your science notes?"

"Did we talk about that when I was asleep? Because I don't remember that."

"I put a note on your tray at lunch, you jelly doughnut! It clearly said: '*Meet me at the swings and give me your science notes.*'"

"Chloe, I didn't get that note. What I did get on my lunch tray, next to my delicious Italian hoagie, was a message from you telling me how much your heart aches for me."

"My love note?! The one Tao gave me!" She began searching her purse. "Where is it?"

"You gave it to me, and apparently I gave it to Paige."

"Paige?" she asked. "I didn't know you liked Paige. I thought you and Jess were going out, but hey, I say go for it. This is exactly the sort of thing those paper dolls deserve." She looked at the folded papers on the table: the paper hockey puck, the science notes, and the love note. "I'll take this," she said, grabbing *My heart aches . . .* "It's *mine*. From Tao." She stormed away, then quickly pivoted on her heels and came back. "I'll take this, too." She snatched the science notes. "I'll bring them back in a little while." She paused. "Thanks." And once again, she stormed away.

When Hurricane Chloe was gone, Ben focused his attention back on me. "And that, Abby, is what we call a *double-decker switch-up*. Chloe didn't know she gave that bad boy to me, and I didn't know I gave it to Paige." He shrugged. "It happens."

I'd answered one question, but not the more important one—the location of the drop. I needed Tao for that. When the hall monitor tried to ask me where I was going, I flashed the pass. It felt powerful to be able to go anywhere.

I felt someone following me and turned to see Logan on my heels.

The scene in the library was too big for him not to catch. "So, Tao gave a love note to Chloe, who gave it to Ben by accident, who then gave it to Paige, also by accident." He thought. "What we don't know is why Tao gave it to Chloe in the first place if he likes Paige. And that's what you want to find out, right?"

"Among other things," I said. Any girl at The Mount would trade their Italian hoagie to spend time with Logan Murphy, and I was not an exception. I liked that he was interested in the quest, even if he didn't really understand it, but I didn't have time to get him up to speed.

He added, "At least that clears things up between Jess and Ben. That's good."

"I guess."

"But the Chloe-Tao-Paige thing is still a problem?"

"Sure."

My phone vibrated in my pocket. Another hot InstaPic was posted. This one was from Jeremy with a note that said:

My boyfriend is pretend

And this was his post:

> **Jeremylovesbugs:** Looky looky what you find when you leave school early for an allergy shot. This little puppy (Oops! Not a real puppy, Shadow) was tied to the string of a balloon that fell out of the sky right into my hot little hand. @The Coffee Station.

1:00pm

CHAPTER 17

And there it was.

My big lie.

My feelings went from hall-pass-powerful to helpless.

I literally slumped over and propped my forehead on a random locker. It felt cool on my burning skin.

"Abs, you okay?" Logan asked.

"No, Logan. I'm terrible. This is a shop door of a day!" I snapped. I seriously thought I might cry.

"Whoa. Um. I don't know what to do with that. Should I call the nurse? 911? Get you a tampon? Give you a hug?"

I straightened up. "No. It's fine. I'm fine. Everything is *fine*!"

"You don't look fine."

"Thanks a lot," I said, but I knew he was right. My makeup had sweated off long ago, and my armpits were soaked.

Logan gave me a hug with his arms squared around me so we didn't really touch. He patted my back. "It'll be okay. Is that what I should say?"

I had to give him points for trying.

"I'm okay. Really." I forced a smile.

My phone vibrated. A text:

Paige: Where are you? We need your help.

What I should've texted back was:

Abby: I'm on my way. I'm having the worst day of my life, but I'm on my way to help you decorate the gym. You can count on me, because I'm that kind of great friend.

Instead: I closed my message app.

"Look, I have to do something. I'll see you later."

I navigated the hallways, moving as fast as I could without running, because not even the magic of a hall pass could make running in the halls permitted.

Logan called from behind me, "I'm not leaving you."

Finally, I reached the cafeteria and instantly spotted Tao sitting by the windows with his gang. Snow was lying on the ground—a solid two inches by now.

"There he is," I said to Logan. When I didn't get an answer, I turned to see he was no longer behind me. I figured I knew where he was. Yup, in the food line, snatching up the very last hoagie.

I finger-combed my hair down to my shoulders, straightened my sweater, stood up straight, smiled, and readied myself to approach Tao's table, but my feet didn't move.

Then, suddenly, a voice next to me asked, "Need a wingman for this?"

It was Shadow.

I did. I really, really did want some company, and of all the people around me, only Shadow seemed to know what I needed. She had some kind of sixth sense.

I nodded.

And she led the way to Tao's table.

"Hey, guys." Shadow took an empty chair, turned it around, and sat on it backward. "S'up?"

Tao said, "Hey, Shadow. What's going on?"

He was always nice to Shadow. In fact, he was nice to everyone. Tao was incredibly likable that way.

"Hi, Abs."

I waved a sweaty palm. My mouth was too dry to form a word.

Shadow said, "We need to talk to you."

"Okay." He got up and brought his fries to an empty table nearby. As he sat, he asked her, "How's pug life?"

"Life's always good at the dog park. You know what I'm sayin'?"

"Sure do." He dipped a French fry in ketchup. It bent as he steered it into his mouth. "So what's going on?"

Shadow looked at me to start the convo.

I swallowed. "You see, Tao . . . um . . . it seems there's this note. It's, um . . . sort of personal. Man, this is awkward."

"What is it, Abs?" He used his fingers to make a little square around himself. "No judgment zone right here. Ask me anything."

See what I mean? He was just so nice.

"Well, this note. There's this note. And it seems that you gave it to Chloe. A . . . um . . . it was a . . ." I couldn't get the words out.

Shadow picked up for me. "A love note. It said, '*My heart aches*' or some other shop door like that. You had it, and you tossed it to Chloe during math this morning. And we don't really care why. We just wanna know where you found the note in the first place."

He rocked back in his chair and made a little blocking move with his hands. "Whoa, whoa, whoa. I tossed that weird thing in the *trash can*. I didn't give anything to Chloe. Okay? Is that what Paige thinks? Is that why she's not returning my texts?"

"'Fraid so," Shadow confirmed.

"Oh man." He shook his head.

"Tao, where did you get it?" I asked. "Like, the exact location. Global positioning satellite coordinates would be helpful."

"Coordinates? No. It was stuck to my test that Jess handed back. I thought she was playing some kind of a joke on me. I didn't get it, so I tossed it in the trash."

"Stuck to your math test?" Shadow asked.

"Yeah. The one Abby got an A-minus on."

Even Tao knew.

Shadow said, "Thanks. That's all we needed." She stood up and turned the chair back around.

"Wait," I said. I was starting to connect some dots. "Mr. Valdez's class, right?"

"Yeah. Right. He's our math teacher. You know that."

I was thinking this through out loud. "He usually takes tests home and grades them and then brings them into class in his briefcase, right?"

"Yeah," Tao said. "That's exactly what he did this morning. He took them out of his briefcase and gave them to Jess to pass out. Or actually, I think she grabbed them. She likes to see everyone's grade."

"So," I said, "the note could've come from Mr. Valdez."

Tao scrunched his forehead. "Pretty sure Valdez's heart isn't aching for me."

"Of course not." I shook my head. "That's not what I meant. Just that he had the note before you did."

"Could be," Tao said. "Look, if there isn't anything else, I really want to talk to Paige and clear this all up."

"You've been super helpful," I said, but instead of moving to leave, I just continued staring at him. "But that's how you are, right? You're nice and helpful and—"

"*Was* there something else?" he asked.

Shadow echoed, "Yeah, Abby, was there something else you wanted to tell Tao?"

2:00pm

CHAPTER 18

On our way back to the gym, we passed a hall monitor, a junior on the debate team. I flashed my magic pass, while Shadow merely nodded. Geez, no way that would work. She was so busted. But he glanced away like he'd never even seen her. Totally ignored her! Hmm . . . maybe I wasn't the only powerful one around here.

"What did you think I was going to say to him?" I asked Shadow on our way back to the gym.

"I don't know, but you looked like you were gonna say something."

"I couldn't come up with anything good on the spot," I said.

"Why would you need to 'come up with' anything?" she asked. "Why don't you just say what's on your mind? Don't you see that that's exactly why you're in this situation? You're afraid to be yourself. That's why you have secrets and lies in the first place. What are you afraid of?"

I didn't want to tell her about AndAbby, so I did what I'd been doing all day: I deflected. "Look who's talking. *Is this yourself?*" I indicated her collar and answered for her, "No. It's something you made up to hide behind. So don't talk to me about being afraid."

We got to the gym, and without responding, she marched away from me. I'd made her mad. Probably not the best move, because there was no predicting what an angry Shadow would do to me today. She didn't understand my situation. She didn't have anything to lose the way I did.

2:05. Just thirty-five more minutes and I could get outside. Finally.

The gym looked really good: hearts lined the stage, bistro tables were covered with red cloths and flower vases, silver glitter sparkled on every surface. Manny had set a hundred chairs up around the perimeter of the gym, and Gordon had dressed every one of them up with tightly curled ribbons. But the arch didn't look quite like the pictures in the Peppermint Twist planner/notebook.

Paige's hair was twisted up and knotted with a pencil. She sat on the floor tying ribbons to wires. Logan stood on a ladder—the kind that could reach the ceiling, but he was only on the fourth rung—and struggled to get the wires to hold on to the doorframe.

"A little more to the left," Jess directed. Then she saw me. "Where have you been?"

I was too preoccupied with worrying what Shadow might blurt out to come up with an excuse. "It looks really good," I non-answered.

Gordon put his hands on his hips and then wiped his forehead after his grueling day of ribbon curling. He assessed the gym. "It really does."

Paige said, "The arch isn't like the picture."

"It looks great just like this," I said. "No one will ever know about that picture."

She got up off the ground, dusted off her butt, and tilted her head to study the balloons. "Maybe you're right, Abs." Then she looked me in the eyes. "I got a text from Tao. He didn't write that note," she informed me. "But you already knew that, didn't you, Abby?"

"I thought—maybe—I mean—What do you mean?"

"He told me that you straightened it all out. That's why you weren't here decorating, right?"

Before I could answer, Shadow called from the stage area, "Makes you wonder who did write it."

Paige said, "That is an excellent question." She hugged me. "But more importantly, thanks, Abby. You're a really good friend for sorting out that it wasn't Tao."

Never before had it felt so lousy to be hugged.

"What's that noise?" Paige asked, releasing me from her embrace.

I put my hand on my stomach. "My stomach. I'm hungry. Sorry. I missed lunch."

Gordon said, "Bummer. It was hoagie day."

"Yeah. I've heard."

❤ ❤ ❤

Jess looked at her watch and said, "I need to get curlers in my hair, like, now. They need four hours to set just right. Ben loves when my hair is wavy."

Paige asked, "You spoke to him?"

Jess said, "Yeah. He explained the whole double-decker switch-up sitch, so we're solid. Did you want to borrow my curling wand?"

"Oh, no thanks. I'm going to straighten it and wear it down."

"Nice," Jess said. "We're gonna meet here before the dance and go in together, right?"

"Sounds good," I said. "Gym door?"

"Yup," Paige agreed.

They straightened up the gym and left with their backpacks.

I leaned on one of the bistro tables with an open notebook and drew a map of the school and the nearby streets. I scanned InstaPic and made dots where I knew notes had been found: the Donut Hole and the Coffee Station.

Then I made a third dot for the faculty parking lot, where Mr. Valdez's car was parked.

That was where I thought this all started. The red ribbon around his antenna this morning. I should've recognized it from the party store balloons.

Mr. Valdez found *My heart aches* and put it in his briefcase, where it somehow stuck to Tao's math test. That was how all this miscommunication started.

I connected the three location dots:

- The Donut Hole (*I lied to my friends*)
- The Coffee Station (*My boyfriend is pretend*)
- The faculty parking lot (*My heart aches*)

They triangulated around one popular local landmark: the Sullivan Mansion.

"Whatcha doing?" Manny asked from behind me.

"Oh, nothing." I shut the notebook and slid it into my backpack. "Just a little homework thing."

Manny said, "I have something for you."

"You do?"

"Yeah." He put a hoagie on the table.

"You're kidding me! I love hoagie day."

"I know. And you looked like you were having a bad day, and I thought maybe you'd be too busy to grab lunch."

"You were right. I'm starving." I unwrapped it and took a huge bite. "Thanks, Manny." I took a second delicious bite, rewrapped it, and put it in my pack.

"That was really thoughtful of you." I gave him a hug and it felt so good.

> ***What I should've said was:*** "You're a special friend to me, Manny. And thanks for the Power Rangers thing."
> ***Instead:*** I held the hug for an extra second.

"Sure thing." Before he walked away, he asked, "You okay, Abby?"

"I will be. I just have to get somewhere and then somewhere else." I looked at my watch—2:40 couldn't come fast enough.

"Parent-teacher conference about the A-minus?" he asked.

Ugh, shop door! I forgot I had to go there at three o'clock. I wouldn't have enough time to go to the Sullivan Mansion before the conference. "Is there anyone who doesn't know about that?"

"Unlikely," he said.

The end-of-day bell finally rang.

"And that's a wrap! See you all in a few hours." Gordon glanced out the window. "Unless this snow ends up canceling the whole darn thing." He left the gym, followed by Logan, who didn't so much as fold up the ladder. I heard Gordon ask him, "So who's the lucky lady? Who's your date?"

Logan put his arm over Gordon's shoulder. "You know, I'm the kind of guy who can't be limited to just one date. I'm going stag so I can dance with all the girls. How about you, my man?"

"I'm the exact same way, Logan. I couldn't pick just one. You know, and break all those other hearts. I'm too sensitive about the feelings of all those girls out there to do that."

"Good man . . ."

I couldn't hear the rest of the conversation.

I hoisted my backpack over one shoulder. "See you tonight?" I asked Manny.

"For sure," he said.

3:00pm

CHAPTER 19

I entered the Coffee Station and saw my mom already sitting with Mr. Valdez.

I said hi to them and pulled a chair out to sit at their table, thinking, *Let's get this show on the road. I've got places to be, notes to find.* But Mr. Valdez said, "You know what, Abby? You actually didn't need to come to this. Sorry, I should've made that more clear."

"I didn't?" That was weird, because I thought I should be able to explain the circumstances of the A-minus.

"Nah," Mr. Valdez said.

"Cool. Then I'm gonna head out. You know, lots to do for the big dance."

"You have plenty of time." Mom looked at her watch. "I ordered some fries for you and your friend. And I'll give you a lift home when we're done."

"What friend?"

Mom pointed to a corner booth: Shadow.

I joined her. "What are you doing here?"

"Are you kidding me? I have to see what these last two notes say. I mean, I have a pretty good idea. And if it is what I think it is, I can't wait to see all this get even worse." Then she added, "For you. Worse for you." She put a fry in her mouth. "Plus, there's food."

"Gee, thanks. Glad I can entertain you. And feed you."

I watched Mom and Mr. Valdez settle into a conversation.

"I need to get to the Sullivan Mansion right away, but I wanna know what they're talking about. I mean, it was one freaking A-minus. This feels a little extra, you know?"

"Your wish is my command." Shadow held up her phone, through which I could hear Mom's and Mr. Valdez's voices.

I asked, "How did you do this?"

"Well, I introduced myself to your mom. I can't believe she hasn't heard of me, by the way. So, I told her we should totally connect on InstaPic, then I took her phone and added myself to her account. While I had her phone, I dialed myself and set the phone down without hanging it up. Presto, we can hear them," she said and then put a finger in front of her lips.

Mom: Looks like a lot of snow is coming. Think they'll cancel the dance?

Mr. Valdez: Unlikely. The roads are well salted, and I'm going over to plow the school parking lot in a little while. I do a little moonlighting when it snows.

Mom: Well, that's handy for the school.

Mr. Valdez: And my friends. It seems like I'm always getting a call to plow someone out of their driveway. Makes me in high demand.

Mom: So, you're like a math teacher and Superman with a snowplow.

Mr. Valdez: (Laughs) Something like that.

Mom: So, was there something you wanted to discuss about Abby?

Mr. Valdez: Abby's great. She's super smart.

Mom: Yeah, she is. Her grades are okay, right?

Mr. Valdez: Better than okay.

Mom: Okay. If she's great and her grades are good, then why did you want to talk to me?

Mr. Valdez: I wanted to talk to you about this morning.

Mr. Valdez reached into his briefcase and rooted around.

Mom: This morning?

Mr. Valdez: Yeah.

He leaned over and searched all through his bag.

Mr. Valdez: Sorry, I can't find it now, but I wanted you to know that I got it.

Mom: *It*?

Mr. Valdez: Yeah. The note.

Mom: Note?

Mr. Valdez: The note you left for me.

My mouth opened. "Ohmigod." I dropped my forehead into my hands. If this wasn't so horrible and sad, it might be comical, but trust me, I wasn't laughing.

Shadow burst out laughing. "*My heart aches* strikes again!"

Mr. Valdez: And I just want to say that this can be tricky. You know, because we're teacher and parent.

Mom: Umm, about this note . . .

"Just hang up. I can't listen anymore. Let's get out of here," I said.

4:00pm

CHAPTER 20

The walk from the Coffee Station to the Sullivan Mansion wasn't far, but the snow was really piling up, so I worked up a sweat trudging through it for what felt like forever.

The mansion was a historical site that no one had lived in for hundreds of years. I thought maybe George Washington had slept there.

"Let's split up and look around," I said.

"Roh-kay, Raggy," Shadow said in a weird dog voice that was unlike her usual pug imitation.

"Huh?"

"You know, like Scooby Doo—they would always split up and look for clues."

I had no idea what she was talking about, and I wasn't in the mood to play cartoon investigator. "Whatever. You go that way," I said to Shadow, so she could cover one side of the house and I could search the other. I scanned the property carefully. Everything I saw was brown—trees or rocks—and white. A red balloon or ribbon would stand out, but I saw nothing.

I took to looking up and searching the trees, and my face was instantly covered with snow. No balloons caught in the trees.

I met Shadow around the back of the house. "Anything?"

She shook her head and shivered. "Maybe we can look more in a little while when the snow lets up. I'm freezing."

I glanced down and saw that her Doc Martens had holes. Her socks were probably soaked and her feet frozen.

"What are we going to do until then?" I asked.

"I don't know, but let's do it inside." She reached for the mansion's back door, which was locked.

"I'll try the front door," I said. I followed my footprints in the snow around to the front, glad I was wearing boots. I tried the knob, but it didn't budge. A second later the front door opened.

It was Shadow.

"How did you do that?" I asked, entering the house.

"Secret. And here's the thing about secrets. They only work if you don't tell anyone." She closed the door behind me.

"I didn't tell anyone my secrets."

Just then we both felt our phones vibrate with a post from InstaPic.

We each looked at our phones. There was a pic of another one of my notes.

"Oh, really?" she asked me. "You didn't?"

This one said,

I have a crush on my
best friend's boyfriend.

"This isn't good for you," Shadow said.

The knot in my stomach that had been there all day tightened. "I'm toast." I put my phone down. "I can't look. What are the comments saying?"

"Want me to read them to you?"

"Okay."

Shadow read:

PeteyMcPete: It's gotta be Jess. She likes Tao.

KittyKatKominsky: But Jess's boyfriend isn't pretend. It's Ben. I saw him today. He's real.

PeteyMcPete: #truth.

SamanthaNickerbocker: After the "pretend boyfriend" note I'm sure these are Shadow's notes. If she has imaginary pugs, why not an imaginary boyfriend? But who's her best friend?

PeteyMcPete: Maybe her best friend is pretend too.

SamanthaNickerbocker: You're a genius. That's got to be it.

KittyKatKominsky: Yup. Makes sense.

"It continues with everyone agreeing it's me," Shadow said. "Well, that's just super. As if I needed another push down the social totem pole at The Mount."

I couldn't tell her how happy that made me. "I'm sorry," I said as sincerely as I could.

"I'm going to set this straight. Right now." She went to type on her phone.

"Oh geez, please don't do that."

"Why should I take the hit for something you did? Something so royally stupid. I mean, really, Abby, what were you thinking?"

I didn't answer her right away. I didn't have a good answer. It seemed like a good idea at the time. I glanced outside at the snow, and I wondered for a second how long we'd be snowed in.

"I'm posting the truth," she said.

"No. Wait. I'll tell you." But then I hesitated. Telling her why I did all this was embarrassing.

She tapped her sloshy boots. "I'm waiting."

> ***What I should've said was:*** Some kind of great lie that could turn all this around, but that didn't exist.

So, what I said was: "It's all about 'AndAbby.'"

She asked, "What does that even mean?"

"You see, over winter break, Jess and Paige went on the tubing trip together. And they got really close and coupled-up with Ben and Tao and did super fun things and had all these inside jokes. So when we got back to school, I was kind of on the outside. I felt like I was going to fall off the back end of JessPaigeAndAbby."

"You have no idea what the outside is like," she said.

"Maybe not the way that you do, but I know I don't want to be there. So I told them things that weren't true about concerts and boots . . . and Fabio."

"You made him up so you could fit in," she clarified.

"It just came out, and once it did, I couldn't seem to backpedal out of it. I figured in a few weeks we'd pretend break up because the long-distance thing wouldn't work for us." I caught her rolling her eyes and added, "We're not so different. You make up stuff too. I mean, you know those pugs aren't real, don't you?"

She bared her teeth a little.

"Why do you do that?" I asked about the growl.

"What?"

"It's like you make yourself weird on purpose. *That* keeps you on the outside." I added, "You don't even try to get inside."

"Maybe I like it here," she said.

"I don't believe that. It's lonely there." I pointed to my collar. "That's why you wanted me to wear this. To join you."

"Maybe you're right. And what better way to get you here with me than to expose you?" Once again she went to start typing.

I had to stop her. "So what if they think it's you? Really, so what?! You're already on the outside. I'm not."

> ***What Shadow should've said was:*** "You're right, Abby. Sure, this sucks, but I'm used to it. I know what it's like here on the outside, and I wouldn't want you to feel this way. You have a nice group of friends, and you shouldn't mess that up. I'll just let people believe it's me."
> ***Instead, what she said was:*** "But you *are* Abby. You have to make up boots and boyfriends to fit in. You *are* on the outside. You're just pretending you're not." Then she added, "The real you already *is* AndAbby."

5:00pm

CHAPTER 21

That stung.

Was she right?

Did I do things to fit in with Paige and Jess that weren't exactly *me*?

> ***What I should've said was anything other than what I did:*** "Don't try to make it sound like we're the same. I have friends. You don't."

As soon as the words were out of my mouth, I wished I could grab them and pull them back.

And that's when it happened.

Shadow: Abby Gray did it. She wrote the notes.

I swallowed and let my head fall into my hands. A little puke inched up my throat.

That was it.

Four words.

Abby

Gray

Did

It.

With four words Shadow ruined my life as I knew it. Four words was all it would take for me to be

Friendless,

Boyfriendless,

Fake-boyfriendless,

Humiliated.

In four words I'd go down in Mount Lebanon Middle School history as a joke. The girl who lied, made up a boyfriend, and crushed on her best friend's boyfriend. And was stupid enough to write these things down and let them float away on balloons, only to be discovered around her school. And then spent an entire day desperately trying to cover up the truth.

It was official: I was "AndAbby."

❤ ❤ ❤

Bright headlights and the sound of a snowplow thundered toward the mansion's front door.

Someone was here!

We went outside to find Mr. Valdez in the driver's seat. He called out the window, "Let's go. There's a dance to get ready for."

We climbed in the front with him. I looked at my phone and watched the comments:

PeteyMcPete: Abby Gray. LOL. Omg. She made up that boyfriend. That's so lame.

KittyKatKominsky: Haha. LMAO. Which one of her best friends' bfs does she love?

SamanthaNickerbocker: I can't wait to get to the dance and watch this catfight.

"What are you doing here?" Shadow asked Mr. Valdez.

I didn't say anything as I watched my life fall apart, one humiliating comment at a time. Then:

Incoming call: Jess Sawyer

Decline

Incoming call: Paige Bakenya

Decline

Incoming call . . .

I turned the phone off.

"You okay, Abby?" Mr. Valdez asked.

Shadow asked, "Yeah, Abby. What's wrong?"

"I'm fine," I said, then I asked Mr. Valdez, "How'd you know we were here?"

"Your mom and Shadow are connected on InstaPic, so she can see where Shadow is, and she knew you left together. I was heading to plow the school parking lot after our meeting, and she asked me if I could get you guys home." He put the truck in gear. "Let's get going."

Shadow asked him, "Are you gonna tell us what happened?"

"With what?"

"With Abby's mom. Do you like her?" she asked.

Maybe I should've been shocked by her assertiveness, but I hardly heard the question. Sounds floated around me like background noise while I imagined everyone laughing at me at the dance tonight. Paige and Jess would de-friend me. I'd officially be on the outside. With Shadow.

Mr. Valdez cleared his throat. "Um, I, um. Hmm. Gee, I'm sorry, Abby. I don't know what I was thinking. It was stupid of me. It's just that there was this note, and I thought . . . I don't know what I was thinking. I didn't mean for things to be this awkward."

"That's not an answer," Shadow said. "Do you like her?"

"Um. That's kind of personal . . ."

Then Shadow said, "I always thought that you and Miss Young would make a nice couple."

"She's a nice lady and we're friends, but we're also colleagues and she has a boyfriend."

That gave me an idea. Maybe. Just maybe Miss Young could be my Hail Mary and provide me with an opportunity to save things. "Are you sure she has a boyfriend? Like, have you met him?"

"Oh, come on, Abby." Shadow must've known what I was thinking . . . that maybe I could peg the notes on Miss Young to get me off this humongous hook—as long as the last note was never found.

I whispered, "It could work."

Mr. Valdez said, "Yeah. He's real. His name is Jake. I've met him. Nice guy."

"Ugh," I said under my breath.

The snow let up, giving Mr. Valdez a much-needed opening to change the subject. "Looks like the snow's moving out just in time for the roads to get cleared for the dance. I'm going to plow the school parking lot one more time to make sure it's good for tonight. It won't take long at all."

"Okay," I said. "Is it okay if I go inside and take care of one last thing in the gym while you do that?"

He pulled up as close to the door as he could. "I'll pick you up here in about fifteen minutes and take you home."

"I'll help you," Shadow said, hopping out of the truck behind me.

6:00pm

CHAPTER 22

"Mom, I'm home!"

She called from upstairs, "I've got the straightener all hot and ready to go for you. Better hurry."

I took a quick shower and contemplated staying home from the dance. Probably Jess and Paige wouldn't be waiting for me at the gym door, and I would have to walk in alone to an attack of stares, laughs, and comments. It would be horrible. But if it wasn't tonight, it would be Monday and I'd have to worry about it all weekend.

Mom came into my room as I finished drying my hair. "So, wanna tell me about your day?"

I looked at her in the mirror.

She knew.

I didn't know exactly what she knew, or how, but she knew I was having a bad day. I sighed, putting the brush down. "I don't really want to talk about it. In fact, maybe I'll just skip the dance."

"Oh, now that's a good idea."

I could scoop the sarcasm up like ice cream.

"You can just ignore whatever is going on and never confront it. That's a good plan, Abs." She started walking out of my bedroom. "I'll make popcorn and you can put on your pajamas."

I said, "Cool. And you can ignore the Mr. Valdez thing at the same time."

"Touché." She started brushing my hair. "You know, I appreciate how open he is. That he's willing to put himself out there and take a risk."

"A risk?"

"Sometimes it's risky to be open and truthful with our feelings. But while it's scary, it might not be so bad." She pulled the straightener down my long hair.

"But it might be bad," I said.

"It might. And if it is, you deal with that. Usually things don't end up as bad as we imagine."

"They could be worse."

"Or they could be better, and you'd never know it if you didn't take that chance."

"Are you going to take a chance with Mr. Valdez?"

"I just might. When he's not your teacher anymore." She straightened a strip of hair, then touched my shoulders. "Are you going to take a chance at the dance?"

7:00pm

CHAPTER 23

My dress was perfect: deep blue, knee length, spaghetti straps. Jess had helped me pick it out. My headband was bedazzled, thanks to Paige.

I walked up the sidewalk toward the entrance to the school gym.

They were standing outside. Paige and Jess, that is.

"Your phone is turned off," Jess said.

"Yeah," I said.

Paige held up a paper. It was the last note. It had fallen and Paige had it. Of course, I knew what it said before I read it: *I love Tao*.

I didn't think it was physically possible for me to feel worse, for my heart to sink any lower into my stomach.

But I did.

And it did.

Although curious, I didn't ask her where she found it. All the balloons had sunk from the sky. Everyone knew everything.

"How could you?" Paige asked.

"How could you?" Jess echoed.

I sighed.

I was out of moves.

I was going to take a risk. "I've had a crush on Tao forever. I just never told you guys, because, well, I thought you'd laugh at me."

"Why would we laugh at you?" Paige asked.

"Because I'm the numbers girl, not the girl who gets the guy. That's you two." I indicated Paige. "You're perfect. Everything you touch is beautified." And then to Jess, I said, "And you're so cool and hip, and you have the best of everything. Of course boys like you. You're 'Paige and Jess,' and I'm just 'AndAbby.'" I used air quotes. "The afterthought."

Jess and Paige looked at each other. I steadied myself for the incoming attack.

I figured what Paige would say was: "Abby, that's it. I can't stand a liar. There's no way we can be friends anymore. Oh, and you're totally out of the decoration committee."

I imagined Jess would say: "You even lied about those boots, didn't you? It just doesn't get any worse than that. Have fun in the dog pound."

But what I imagined was totally and completely wrong. ***What happened was:***

"You're *not* an afterthought, Abs," Paige said.

"I'm sorry if I ever made you feel like 'AndAbby,'" Jess said.

They weren't mad?

They didn't hate me?

They weren't putting me on the outside?

It didn't seem real. Were they joking with me? Maybe there was going to be some bigger humiliation they'd planned after this false sense of security?

"What?" I asked.

"And if I'm being honest," Paige added, "I always kind of thought the boyfriend was fake, but I didn't really care."

"Yeah. Me too," Jess said. "I mean, *Fabio Risotto*? Not really believable. Just sayin'."

I let out a relieved snort-giggle-tear combo.

Then they walked over and embraced me in a three-way hug.

Paige said, "Remember during winter break when we did that No Regrets thing? We're supposed to keep what we wrote down a secret, but I'm going to tell you. I wrote down that I regretted that you weren't with us, Abby."

Jess said, "You did not."

"I did," Paige said.

"I did, *too*!" Jess said.

That's when we saw something else floating in the sky.

It wasn't snow.

CHAPTER 24

A storm of red balloons began to fall. We grabbed them.

"There are notes tied to them." Jess reached up and waited for one to fall into her hand.

Paige asked, "Oh no, what now, Abby? There's more?"

"Not from me. I have no more secrets," I said.

Chloe got out of her parents' car, snatched a ribbon, and unfolded a note as she walked over to us. "It says, '*It's always been Abby*.'"

Other kids got dropped off in the parking lot, each picking up a ribbon on their way to the gym door and reading. Gordon's said, "*I wish Abby Gray was my girlfriend*."

Logan's said, "*I'm dancing with Abby tonight.*"

One finally landed in Jess's fist. She unfolded it. "*Abby is the one*," she read.

Ben hopped out of the back of his parents' car and checked things out on his way to the door. "Now everyone is sailing notes away on balloons? I guess I missed the memo."

"Who did this, Abby?" Paige asked.

I was at a complete loss.

Who would do this?

Who had these thoughts about me?

I was someone's secret crush?

I stuttered a little, "I—I—I don't . . ."

Someone was crushing on *me*. The thought of this made me uncomfortable and tingly and sweaty and heart-racy and self-conscious and curious . . . and . . . and . . . just so happy, because actually—

"I know who."

He had been there the whole time.

Right in front of me.

All day.

For years.

Shadow whispered to me, "If you did this . . . I mean, you're just digging a deeper hole."

"No. I didn't. And, geez, don't even suggest that. Besides, I've been with you all day." I looked at the sky and mentally calculated. "With the wind like this, the only way these could have dropped right here, right now, would be with incredible precision. It would take a good math head. And also, someone knew I wrote the notes *before* Shadow's InstaPic message outed me."

Jess asked, "How is that possible? No one knew it was you."

"Someone did. Someone who knows me better than anyone else," I said.

Just then a body emerged from the wintry darkness.

I knew who it was before anyone could see him.

"Manny."

I met him in the parking lot.

"You. You did this?"

He smiled. "Guilty."

"But how did you know?"

"I've known all day. The creases in *My heart aches* . . . I know them. I'm the one who taught you how to make an origami frog. You loved frogs and I showed you, remember? We were in my tree house. First grade."

I got a little teary as the memory flooded back to me. "I remember. You kissed me and asked me to be your girlfriend."

"Right. You thought that the kiss meant we had to get married," he reminded me.

I held up *It's always been Abby.* "And this? Is it true or just a fantastic distraction to get the heat off me?" Either would be great, but now outside the school gym in the snow, I really hoped it was true.

Why was I secretly crushing on anyone?

Why did I invent Fabio, when Manny was right here the whole time?

How could I be so smart and so dumb?

"Abby, it's always been you." He took my hand. "But you're wrong about something in the tree house."

What had I remembered wrong? "I am?"

"Yes. That's when I kissed you *for the first time.*"

"Was there another time?" I asked.

"There will be," Manny said.

And then he did it. Kissed me, that is.

I was so wrapped up in that amazing, wonderful, wintry kiss that I hardly noticed my classmates around me cheering and clapping.

Jess and Paige let out a collective "aww."

8:00pm

CHAPTER 25

"Welcome to Peppermint Twist!" Mr. Valdez shouted from the gym door, and everyone piled inside. Manny took my hand and led me to the door, but I pulled him back.

"Wait a sec," I said.

"What?"

"Two things." I started, "I should have known. You were right there all this time, and I wasn't paying attention. I'm sorry I didn't see. It's all so obvious to me now, Manny. Of course it's you."

"There's a lot of distraction in this place." He craned his neck to indicate the school. "That was one thing. What's the second?"

I leaned in to kiss him again.

When I pulled away, he looked down at me. "I like the second thing."

That's when we saw one of the last kids to arrive at the dance getting out of his car: Tao.

He walked to the door. "Hi, Abs," he said, not taking his eyes off the ground.

Manny took a step away from me. "I'll wait over there," he said to me and gave Tao a guy-nod.

I said, "Tao, uh. Oh . . . uh . . . I . . . err. Geez, this is awkward."

"You think?" he asked, made eye contact with me, and let out a little nervous laugh, which was exactly what was needed to break the tension.

"Yeah. Very. I'm sorry I embarrassed you," I said.

"Me? Nah, I'm fine. But are you okay?" Even after all this crap, he was still nice. Paige was lucky.

"I'm actually better than okay. Seems that I was so fixated on one thing, I didn't see something else." I looked at Manny, who packed a snowball and threw it at Logan, who darted one right back at him.

"Good thing you didn't miss it," Tao said and headed to the door. "Coming in?"

"Oh yeah. It's freezing out here."

"See you inside," Tao said.

I met Manny at the door.

"How was that?" he asked.

"Not as bad as I'd imagined. One more question: How'd you calculate that? The landing here at just the right time? You'd have to have thought of every variable perfectly—wind, snow, temperature, rate of sinkage—"

"Or I could have filled them only a tiny bit and let them go from right over there a minute ago. Simple. No calculations," he said.

Then Manny took my hand and we went to the dance, but when we entered the gym, things didn't look exactly the way we'd left them after school.

I stood next to Paige. She scanned the gym, and her mouth hung open. Twinkly white garden lights had been hung from the ductwork, giving the whole room the feel of a wintry wonderland.

Principal Rashed and a lady walked over to me. "Abby Gray." His voice was deep and always sounded angry.

"Yes?"

"Which one is Bakenya?"

Paige lifted a hand. "That's me."

"You're the head of the committee that did all this?"

"Yes. I am."

He said, "I'd like to introduce you to Dr. Degnan. She's the superintendent of our school district."

Dr. Degnan was a petite woman in a red-and-white-striped dress that was perfectly fitting for the occasion.

"Hello, Miss Bakenya," she said to Paige.

"I like your dress," Paige said.

"Why, thank you. But all this." Dr. Degnan looked around the gym. "I had no idea what pop art was, so I looked it up. And I'm pretty sure this isn't it."

"Oh, right," Paige said. "About that—"

"But you have quite an eye for decor." She glanced around again. "Great job."

Paige said, "I'm glad you like it."

Then Dr. Degnan pointed behind Paige. "I especially love that. It's like the *crème de la crème* of dance *accoutrements*."

Paige turned around (we all did) to see what the superintendent was raving about.

Everyone was stunned at the sight: the balloon arch over the door had been rejiggered to match Paige's drawing in her Peppermint Twist planner.

"I don't know how you did that, but it's spectacular." Then Dr. Degnan said, "I'm going to get some punch. Again, well done, Paige."

"Thank you," Paige said, but her eyes didn't leave the arch.

Principal Rashed gave us a thumbs-up and followed Dr. Degnan.

"How did this happen?" Jess asked.

"Well, I know you were really disappointed that it didn't work out the way you'd imagined. And I'd been thinking about it all day, trying to figure out an equation for the measurements of the wire frame to fit just right. And we kept trying to get the balloons to tie tightly to the frame, but Shadow had such good luck sticking the cut-out hearts on the stage with the masking tape, I figured that we could just do that all around the doorframe. You know, keep it simple," I said.

"So, you came back and did this all by yourself?" Jess asked.

"Not by myself. I had help." I pointed to Shadow, who was sitting in the corner with Gordon Chang. She'd pulled a few other chairs in a semicircle around her and set a Milk-Bone on each.

Paige pointed to the white lights. "But how did you do those?"

"They're fabulous," Jess said.

"Way fab," I agreed. "But that wasn't me. I don't know who did that."

"Maybe Fabio Risotto?" Jess asked jokingly.

CHAPTER 26

Gordon escaped Shadow's paws and took a place at the podium in front of the gym. He slapped on a pair of Beats headphones, opened his laptop, and bent the microphone down. Dance music flooded the gym.

Logan was the first to start flossing. Then we all started dancing. I couldn't believe how things worked out. I mean, what was the probability? I paused to mentally calculate the statistics and standard deviation, but I stopped my math when I saw Shadow still sitting with the Milk-Bones.

> ***What I could've done was:*** Dance with my friends and be thankful that the day ended up as good as it had.
> ***Instead:*** I pushed my luck.

"I'll be right back," I said to Manny and walked into the boneyard.

I said to Shadow, "Come on. Dance with me."

She said, "You didn't learn anything about being on the outside, did you?"

"I learned that you don't need to be." I took her hand and dragged her to the dance floor, whispering something to Gordon on my way past him.

Paige and Jess looked at us.

"There's another secret I have to tell you," I said to them.

They stopped dancing.

"Shadow and I are friends. And she's going to hang out with us. Be part of our group, that is."

Before they could answer or object, Gordon blared "Who Let the Dogs Out?" And we all jammed.

The End

Excerpt from

THE GIRL WHO RUINED CHRISTMAS

A TWEEN HOLIDAY NOVELLA

CINDY CALLAGHAN

CHAPTER 1

If you search for images of "teen locked in Harper Hollow Falls jail," you'd see a picture of thirteen-year-old Brady Bancroft in soaked Chuck Taylors and frozen Hello Kitty socks. The expression on her face would say, "This whole town hates me."

That girl would be me.

I'm Brady Bancroft.

CHAPTER 2

A week earlier: November 27

Me and my best friend Lou Lou sip bubble tea and scope out the best place to plant ourselves on the beach.

"Here?" I ask and point to a spot near a group of sandcastle builders.

Lou Lou faces toward the sun as if "trying on" this spot, because it might somehow feel different than another spot. "Yup. Good." She spreads her blanket and notices me eying the struggling castle sculptors.

I ask her, "Should I?"

"They do look like they need you."

I drop my beach bag and hand Lou Lou my tea. I approach the castle makers and offer, "I could give you a hand . . ."

When the man nods I help myself to a nearby icing spatula, and in a few flicks of my wrist I've smoothed and rounded the turret perfectly into shape.

I accept his thanks and return to my towel and tea.

Lou says, "You're like a superhero."

Taking my position to bask in the warm southern California sun, I brag, "One of my many talents."

Before closing my eyes to catch a snooze so that my vocal cords will be well rested for a cappella group practice later, I see Allie Moskowitz—Orange County Junior High's "it girl"—leave the Venice Beach sidewalk and head in our direction.

She's holding a remote-controlled gadget in one hand, while a second gadget flies overhead.

"Hi, Allie," I say.

"Hi, girls." She flashes her bright smile. As far as It Girls go, Allie is one of the good ones.

"What's that?" Lou asks.

"Oh my gosh, the latest. Isn't it amaze? It can take aerial pictures and send them right to my phone."

Lou asks, "Lemme see."

"Oh, I'm not taking pictures right now, silly. But I could, if I wanted to."

I ask, "What do you want to take pictures of?"

Allie sighs. "I'm not really into taking pictures."

Me and Lou Lou exchange a look of confusion.

"Then what's it for?" I ask.

Allie says, as if the answer is totally obvious, "To *have*."

My pause tells her that I don't understand.

"Just to have. You know what they say, the one who dies with the most toys wins."

I sort of nod. And notice Allie salivating over the sight of my purple-green drink a quarter of the way filled with popping boba.

"Don't even tell me that's the new lavender flavor."

"It is. Want to try?"

Allie takes the cup and sips. "Mmm. Best. Invention. Ever."

"Better than that?" I indicate her remote thing.

"Tough call. Luckily, we don't have to choose. We can have them both, right?" Then Allie says, "See you tonight at practice," and we watch her walk back toward the sidewalk.

"She took your drink," Lou Lou says.

"I know."

Lou Lou hands me her drink. "I woulda done the same thing."

I sip Lou's chocolate tea-based drink and set it between us in the sand.

Our eyes follow Allie as she walks along staring at her phone, drinking my drink, her hover camera over her head, oblivious that she's stepping on people's towels and into kids' sand projects.

"Is she horrible?" I ask.

"Only mildly." Lou tilts her head. "And not on purpose, I think."

"I'm so jelly of her," I confess.

"Me too," Lou says.

We share a laugh at how stupid it is to be jealous of Allie, and then Lou asks, "So, New York State?

"Yeah. Just two days. My dad has to meet some businesspeople. Me and Mom are tagging along. A little pre-Christmas fam time."

"I'm sure your posts will look fab, and Allie will be jelly of you."

"I'll do my best."

CHAPTER 3

The airport smells like a pine tree forest. There must be twenty fresh trees. A group of children dressed in matching elf outfits stand in three neat rows and belt out "We Wish You a Merry Christmas." Overhead, a man scales the wall in a safety harness, changing the date on a giant calendar to November 28.

My dad collects our suitcases from the baggage carousel while my mom paces around, hugging herself to keep warm.

"I thought Christmas countdown calendars started in December," I say, watching the Spiderman do his job.

"It gets pushed earlier every year," Mom says. "You know they wanted to start the bazaar this weekend, but

I insisted they wait until I get back. I mean, after all, I *am* the chairwoman this year."

In a few minutes, Dad has not only loaded a luggage cart but also obtained the keys to a rental car. He says, "All set," just in time to rescue me from Mom telling me again about the honor of being head of the Christmas bazaar.

The SUV is right out front of the airport. I sit in the car with the heat blasting and watch Dad load the luggage while Mom opens her bags to layer herself with sweater after sweater . . . adding a scarf, a coat, another scarf, and, finally, mittens and earmuffs.

She tries to get into the front seat, but she can't fit because she's bundled herself up so much. "Rob," she calls to my dad, who has added the address into the GPS. "A little help."

Dad comes around the car, moves Mom's seat all the way back and tilts it so that she's practically in my lap.

"Thanks, honey," she says as she lies in the passenger seat.

Not five minutes later, we pass a sign that says

HARPER HOLLOW FALLS, NEW YORK,
POPULATION 1,101.

"Tell me again why we're here?" I ask.

"This is your father's biggest deal ever, Brady. It could change his career." Mom takes off her earmuffs and one of the many scarves.

"I thought you already had a great career," I say. "Aren't you Mr. Real Estate?"

Mom answers for him (she always answers for him), "He is, but now he could be the King of Real Estate. Couldn't you, honey?" Before Dad can speak, she says, "He totally can." She unzips her coat and reaches for the temperature control, but she's too constrained by her outfit for her hand to reach the knob. "Rob, can you lower this a bit? It's stifling."

Dad turns the knob.

I point to the windshield, which is being splatted by tiny white particles falling from the sky. "What the heck?" The particles connect into bigger, fluffier white flakes. "I've never seen snow!"

"We're about as far north as New York goes, practically in Canada," she says. "Lots of snow here."

"Awesome. It's so pretty."

"Brady, maybe you don't truly understand snow," she says. "Why do you think so many people live in California?"

"I don't know how anyone could hate something so white and fluffy."

"You say that now." Then Mom adds, "But, don't worry, we'll be back in the Golden State in a few days for the Christmas bazaar. Being the chairwoman? Sure, it's a lot of work, but it's an honor, really. Are you going to help? We could use it. And maybe Lou Lou too?"

"I'll ask her," I say, but I know Lou Lou won't want to. Last year we helped out with the bazaar by setting up a row of twenty pink artificial Christmas trees in the school gym. They were aluminum and gave us little cuts on our hands.

Dad stops the rental SUV outside of the Yuletide Bed & Breakfast, a big stone Colonial house with a Christmas wreath already hung on every window.

I step out of the toasty car, look up, and open my mouth to let flakes in. "I love snow!"

Mom puts her earmuffs back on. "Come on. Let's go inside." She hustles to the front door and calls back to Dad, "Rob, can you get our bags, honey?"

I fling my backpack on my shoulder and follow.

The smell of chocolate chip cookies permeates the walls of the B&B and sails right up my nose. *Mmmmm.* Meanwhile, snowflakes accumulate into a dust-like layer on the ground and on the holly bushes that stand on either side of the front door.

Before Mom can knock, the door flies open.

"Come in. Come in. You must be the Bancrofts," says a short woman with rosy cheeks and a spotted apron. She holds the door open for my dad, who's struggling with our luggage.

"You need a hand with that?" asks a man in a neon-green tracksuit, walking vigorously up a driveway lined with lantern lights. His arms swing in synch with his giant strides, speed-walking style. "Let me." He takes a leather duffel bag off my dad's shoulder and a briefcase out of his hand. "I'm Kenny, Kenny Crispin. My wife Carmella and I own this here B&B. You've picked the best time of year to come to Harper Hollow Falls. We're all about Christmas. The mistletoe gets hung before Thanksgiving."

The woman, Carmella Crispin, closes the door behind us once Kenny, Dad, and the luggage are inside. She wraps her arms around herself, and excitedly says, "Oooo, it's starting to get cold."

"Dreadfully cold," Mom adds, less enthusiastically.

"I love it," Kenny says. "The colder, the better. That's what I say."

Mom finds the fireplace and positions her butt a few inches away from it without making it appear as though she's toasting her buns.

I look around the house. Kenny Crispin wasn't kidding about Christmas. We still had leftover Thanksgiving turkey in the fridge at home—I mean, it was two days ago—but the Crispins' tree is up and fully trimmed. White lights twinkle in every built-in bookshelf and nook of the B&B.

"Your decorations are great," I say. "I like this one." I indicate a countdown-to-Christmas figurine. Today it reads twenty-eight.

"Thank you, dear," Carmella Crispin says. "It might still be November, but I just get so excited, I can't stand it. My favorite thing to do every day is switch the number." Then she adds, "Maybe I'll let you do it tomorrow." She's visibly giddy with anticipation.

"That'd be cool," I say. "We don't have one of those."

"I can show you the most darling little shop where they make them." Then Carmella Crispin asks Mom and Dad, "What brings you to our little hollow?"

"Business," Mom says, indicating Dad.

"What kind of business you in?" Kenny Crispin asks Dad.

Mom answers for him. Dad knows Mom loves to talk, and since he doesn't, they're kind of a perfect couple. "He's in real estate. He's here to look at Schneider's Tree Farm for development."

The smiles instantly drain from Kenny and Carmella's rosy-cheeked faces. Either they have no idea what Mom is talking about, or they have every idea and don't like it. Mom adds, "For a factory."

Kenny says flatly, "We know."

"We've heard," Carmella says.

"The Schneiders are dear friends of ours." Kenny picks up the bags and turns to bring them up the curved staircase.

"Then they must've told you how good this will be for your town?" Mom asks. "Create jobs."

Carmella clears her throat. "Let's not talk about it." Then she straightens up, seeming to flip an internal switch that reignites the sparkle in her eyes. She faces me. "I'll show you to your room, and we can head out to see Ol' Sturdy Stan McSpruce."

"Who's that?" I ask.

"Ol' Sturdy isn't a 'who,' it's a 'what,'" Kenny Crispin explains from the bottom step with a festive giggle.

“The pride and joy of Harper Hallow Falls,” Carmella adds. “Something very special is happening tonight in the town square, where Ol’ Sturdy Stan stands.”

“What?” I ask. “What’s happening?”

“Now, you don’t want me to spoil the surprise,” Carmella says.

Kenny adds, “That would be like opening a present before Christmas.”

ABOUT THE AUTHOR

Cindy Callaghan is best known for her book *Just Add Magic* and its sequel, *Potion Problems*, which are the basis for the Emmy-nominated Amazon Original live-action series *Just Add Magic*. She is also the author of the middle-grade novels *Lost in London, Lost in Paris, Lost in Rome, Lost in Ireland* (formerly titled *Lucky Me*), and *Lost in Hollywood*. Her other works include: the award-winning *Sydney Mackenzie Knocks 'Em Dead, Saltwater Secrets* (which is set up at a major studio), and, most recently, *The Girl Who Ruined Christmas*. Cindy lives in Wilmington, Delaware.

Author photo © Lighteous Photography

SELECTED TITLES FROM SPARKPRESS

SparkPress is an independent boutique publisher delivering high-quality, entertaining, and engaging content that enhances readers' lives, with a special focus on female-driven work. www.gosparkpress.com.

The Girl Who Ruined Christmas: A Tween Holiday Novella, Cindy Callaghan, $12.95, 9781684631155. When a California girl gets stuck in upstate New York for the holiday season, a clean teen, sweetly romantic Christmas adventure perfect for fans of Netflix's *Dash & Lily* ensues.

The Blue Witch: The Witches of Orkney, Book One, Alane Adams. $12.95, 978-1-943006-77-9. Nine-year-old Abigail Tarkana has a problem: her witch magic has finally come in, but it's *different*—and being different is a problem at the Tarkana Witch Academy. Together with her scientist-friend Hugo, she face off against sneevils, shreeks, and vikens in a race to discover the secrets about her mysterious magic.

Tree Dreams: A Novel, Kristin Kaye. $16.95, 978-1-943006-46-5. In the often-violent battle between loggers and environmentalists that plagues seventeen-year-old Jade's hometown in Northern California, she must decide whose side she's on—but choosing sides only makes matters worse.

Wendy Darling: Volume 1, Stars, Colleen Oakes. $17, 978-1-94071-6-96-4. Loved by two men—a steady and handsome bookseller's son from London, and Peter Pan, a dashing and dangerous charmer—Wendy realizes that Neverland, like her heart, is a wild place, teeming with dark secrets and dangerous obsessions.

But Not Forever:A Novel, Jan Von Schleh. $16.95, 978-1-943006-58-8.When identical fifteen-year-old girls are mysteriously switched in time, they discover the love that's been missing in their lives. Torn, both want to go home, but neither wants to give up what they now have.